Secrets

From the Top

Caroline's Journal

The Beginning

by Mr Darcy

Contents

The time was now

She stood lingering...

Within the frame of the open wooden balcony door

Her naked form

Exposed to the crisp cool morning breeze

Taking in the scene and atmosphere

As her gaze wandered to the body

That lay limp and exhausted in the dishevelled sheets

From the night's rapturous entangling

She stood in admiration...

After the many years of a fast-paced career...

With all longing and desires tossed to the wayside

She had finally taken control of her lust-filled fantasies

It was now time for a new era

Passions will now be answered to...

Her gluttonous palate to be satiated

It was time to alleviate her hunger

For she is now the hunter, delicately plucking her prey

She stood alone...

And a smile formed on her swollen pink lips,

Plump from the insatiable appetite that the

Stranger in the bed possessed

Her mind lost in reverie as she lingered on

The night before...

She had taken what she wanted...

Without regret...

Without hesitation...

In a ravenous frenzy

She stood changed...

For she had been ablaze at the idea of

Having him...

Tasting him...

Greedily consuming all his body had to offer and then some...

It caused her thighs to quiver and her juices to seep

From the deep caverns between

She stood empowered...

She had placed him on his knees,

Her hands entwined within the locks of his hair,

Positioning him before her as her aching swollen lips glistened...

Beseeching him to sample her tangy flavours

Causing him to salivate and beg for more

Recognize...

Acknowledge...

Appreciate...

She stood awakened

By Robin LeOra

Chapter 1.
Paris

Caroline is a high-flyer, a CEO of a large company in central London. She has an office the size of a normal house and all the luxuries life has to offer. She was the boss at work and everyone who worked under her knew her loyalties were with them. She wasn't the typical CEO. She, of course, made her company the main focus; it was what she was employed to do. However, she was loyal and adamant about the well-being of the staff that worked on her floor. They were more like family than employees. She had taken her time in her career to find the right balance for work and her colleagues. She never once set them deadlines to keep to; she knew they would work hard and get it all done when it was needed. But for the way she treated them she knew that they wouldn't just do the work to an adequate standard, they would go above and beyond. She would never go into a meeting on the back of their work knowing that something out of the blue would come up and put her on the back foot and having to make concessions to the other party.

She treated them on a daily basis and knew for the love she showed them that she would always have the best from them in return. The door was always open to them, no matter what, work or personal, she was always there for them and would put meetings off to try and help them out if needed. Her staff always came first as she relied upon them on the daily so, she thought, *'If I need to rely on them, I need to be there in the same way for them.'*

Her days were always full, but she always made sure that she had time for a morning meeting with them all and if things needed to be fixed in the office, it was always taken care of. No one in the office had complaints about each other and they always knew that each one of them was only a call or email away and everyone would be there to help.

The business was doing well when Caroline joined it and had gone from strength to strength and she now had business dealings all over the globe. The company bought into failing or cash-strapped companies and breathed new life into them, with the expert oversight of Caroline.

She always made sure that the businesses that they dealt with knew that her focus was on the welfare of the employees of the company. She was highly aware that if you had them on board, then they would thrive. Many of the companies she met with wouldn't accept this or take it on board.

Every time this happened, Caroline would walk away from the deal and just sit and wait for the companies to go to the wall. She would then walk in and her company would buy it outright and turn it around. She was ruthless in her profession; she excelled in every aspect. However, with all of her business dealings and work that she was doing, she was missing something in her life, and this year she was determined to rectify it.

This was *her* year to find happiness or at least explore everything she could. She had decided that the first steps of her new adventure had to be taken away from home, away from all her friends and family. It was going to be her first chance to at least find some happiness and to be the one in charge of her life.

She wanted everything to be on her terms and not anyone else's. She was tired of people thinking she was just a pretty face and always trying to be a piece of meat on someone's arm. She had come to the stage in her life where this wasn't going to happen anymore, and this was going to be the time to turn the tables on convention.

All of Caroline's past relationships had been the same, comfortable but not inspiring. She liked to read and that's all she seemed to do in her relationships. There was no spark left in them, so she sorted out her feelings in books. She had so many things she wanted to do but one thing always came to mind - a masquerade ball somewhere romantic.

She had always envisioned it with whomever she was dating at the time, but with her work schedule so packed, when one came up, she was always away on business or was single. She was looking through the news and internet, searching things for work, when at the bottom of the page, the last few tickets available for the masquerade ball in the Grand Hotel in Paris popped up. This was her chance. She looked at her work schedule and was free the day before and after it. She called her P.A. on the phone.

"I am going away next weekend. Clear my diary and book a ticket for this event, a hotel and flights. Do not book anything in for that time."

Elizabeth emailed all her staff and let them know Caroline would be unavailable for the next weekend. She called her back to inform her the plans were set and telling her to enjoy herself. The ticket confirmation came through that afternoon in Caroline's inbox.

A shopping spree came to mind as it was only three days away and she was planning to get there a day early. So, shopping it was before she left for her adventure, and anything she forgot she would pick up in Paris when she arrived.

It was the night of the masked ball in Paris and Caroline had arrived in the city a day early to make sure she had everything in place for her first-ever masquerade ball. She had been dreaming of this sort of thing for a long time and was getting more and more excited by the minute. She hadn't stopped thinking about it since she had seen the advert for tickets for sale. It was a bit more expensive than she had wanted to spend but she had to jump at the chance.

She spent the day just wandering around the streets of Paris, window shopping and just basking in the City of Love's atmosphere.

She couldn't help but to take it all in and gaze around at the people in the shops and streets, wondering if they were going to be at the ball as well. She watched couples walking hand in hand and she pictured them in matching gowns and tuxedos and doing the tango or foxtrot or any dance that had their bodies close together.

She spotted a man, handsome, built like he was a personal trainer, 'No…' she thought, 'an athlete.' His shoulders were broad, with the muscles under his neck bulging out of the collar of his shirt. His chest was massive and tight; his arms were the sort that if he was holding you close you would feel safe, secure and protected. She could see the tribal tattoos on each arm running down and poking out underneath his sleeves. His jeans fitted well and were tight around his thighs and butt. She followed him around the store to get a better look. She could imagine what he would wear that night if he was going to the ball. Lost in her thoughts, she gasped as he turned around and noticed it wasn't just his muscles that she was captivated by. She had zeroed in on the bulge at the front of his jeans and couldn't help but wonder what having him would feel like. She decided to quit drooling over the mystery man and move on with her day.

Caroline stood about five foot, five inches tall, barefoot. She had a slight but curvy figure; she was toned and didn't weigh more than one hundred and twenty pounds. Her shoulder-length blonde hair flowed gently to her shoulders and those eyes, they were a hypnotic shade of blue that could change colour, depending on her mood.

They could shift from the dazzling blue to an emerald green that would melt a guy's heart by just looking into them. But her eyes could enchant anyone, male or female. Her gaze was captivating. She was a petite firecracker and as gorgeous as anyone could be. She shone like the purest diamond and would light up any room she entered.

She was the director of a company and her job was challenging, pushing her to always be at her best, yet it was rewarding, and she loved it. But this situation was out of her comfort zone entirely; this was not her boardroom. She was in uncharted territory.

She had bought a new dress and shoes for the event. She selected a flowing red dress with a sensational split on the left-hand side that went all the way up to just under her waist. She knew it would show a good deal of leg and not leave much to the imagination. That was her intent, after all. It didn't matter if she showed off her figure in public, as she was in a new city and no one would know her. Plus, the mask would also protect her identity.

The shoes to match her dress were pointed-toe, five-inch heels, black with red soles and with solid platinum snakes on the heel. Their eyes were embedded with rubies and the body of the snake wrapped around the stiletto's spiked heel. She had also, of course, bought new lingerie to finish off the look.

The dress was laying on the bed; it was something a temptress would wear, and that was what she planned on being for the night. Looking back on it now, it was the cut of the dress that got her to purchase it, to send out a signal. She decided to

take a long soak in the bath and relax and look
forward to the evening ahead.

Caroline eased into the bath, while enchanting
music played quietly in the background. She laid
back, closing her eyes and drifting into thoughts of
what was to become of a single lady in Paris. A lady
alone at a masquerade ball in such an inviting,
sensual dress, that left nothing to the imagination
as it clung to all her curves and was made of the
thinnest fabric. It was thin enough to the point that
it was almost a second skin.

The radio station that she was listening to
became moodier and a little darkish in its playlist.
Her thoughts gathered in her mind, she let the music
take hold of her soul. It was as if she could feel
someone's touch on her through the dress right there
and then. Her breathing quickened and she could feel
hands running all over her body as if she was in a
film with her being the only lady left. Everyone
wanted her, it seemed. Her imagination was running
wild as she could sense herself coming close to

having to release the energy inside her that had built up for so long. She thought she felt the sliding sensation of hands all over her body, it felt so real. Out of nowhere, a thrust so deep inside her sent a rip of pleasure through her body. She could feel every inch going into her as her thoughts ramped up. Was it the city she was in? Or was her mind just going to places that she longed to be? It had been so long since she had been with someone, that the images, the sensations, and the touches felt real to her.

Her back arched as she could feel someone taking her deep and hard inside. She swore she could feel the breath on her skin and could sense the overwhelming desire for her body to let go. Her eyes flew open; she was alone again in the candlelit room, still in the bath listening to the same station.

Was it the music that sent her there in her mind? Or was it the guy she had seen in the store who had sent her to the most erotic and surreal thoughts she was having? She didn't know for sure, but she loved the feeling it was giving her, and she was embracing each and every moment.

She decided to take a nap so she could calm herself down. She poured a glass of wine and lay down on the welcoming mattress of her bed. She reread her invite while drinking the wine and a smile came over her face. The realisation hit her that it was tonight, it was all happening tonight. She couldn't wait.

Caroline woke up, startled, as she had thought she had overslept, but she had only been out for about half an hour. She decided she was going to shower and then take her time getting ready. She ordered room service before her shower as she thought to herself that it's a once in a lifetime trip, and she was going to max out the experience and go all out.

Caroline sat down, ate, had another glass of wine and then showered. Once she had washed and relaxed, she started from the top to the bottom of her look. She wanted everything right. Her nails had already been done at the salon while out shopping. She had them extended, with tips filed to a point on each finger and painted glittering silver to match the snakes on her heels. Her lightly tanned skin glowed as she applied body cream all over. It shimmered in the light, enhancing her features. She had to let it dry so as not to get it onto her dress. The bottle said 30 minutes drying time. She wasn't taking any chances; she walked around her room for an hour, air-drying naked to make sure it was set.

The music was still playing in the background and was the same moody tempo she had heard in the bath. She danced around the room listening to the music and noticed her hands had been exploring her body the whole time without even realising what she was doing. They glided over her ample breasts; her nipples had grown hard from her touch. It was as if someone had taken control of her hands and was using them on herself for his pleasure. Her breathing was fast, and she couldn't catch her breath.

Caroline got to the radio and turned it off. She stopped and regained her composure once again.

'What is happening to me?' She hadn't felt this way in a long time. It must have been the city, or the couples, or perhaps even the guy that had captivated her so much she had already felt him spread her wide as he entered her while in the bath. She took a deep breath.

It was time to get dressed; the matching lingerie was red, G-string bottoms, with a matching bra. She took the dress out of its bag and placed it back onto the bed, placing the shoes next to the bed, so they were ready when the time had come. She hadn't had all of it on at the same time before and this was it. She carefully slid the dress over her head and down along her body.

It was form-fitting as she walked to the full-length mirror and took a look. She loved it, all apart from the lines being left by the expensive lingerie. She moved it around in an attempt to make it less intrusive but to no avail. She stood back, taking a moment to decide what to do.

She had no time and no choice. She wasn't going to be able to wear any of it. It had to come off. The only saving grace, she thought, was it still had the label on, so it could go back to the store once she was back in England.

On went the dress again, but as she slipped it over this time, the look and the fit were spot-on. Every inch of the dress clung to her curves. Nothing was left to the imagination. The top hugged her tightly around her ample, heaving breasts. She realised her nipples were on full display, not just when they were erect and solid, but you could see every pimple around the nipples and how large the areola was. She could even see how dark her nipples were, but she didn't care. No one knew her there and the mask would cover her face and give her the confidence to go out and live out her dreams. She slipped on the shoes and grew five inches instantly.

The slit was now able to flow open as the dress was no longer running against the floor.

Each stride showed off the flawless curves of her well-toned legs. The slit stopped just short of showing her glistening, shaven lips and she knew that if she took too big a stride that she would bare all to the world. Her heart raced and her smile was spreading by the second. She carefully placed the mask against her face and at that moment, she stopped being the CEO of a powerful firm and transformed into the new, take-charge-of-her-life, Caroline.

She took a deep breath as all of her emotions that had been building up over time and the sensations she had been having all day, made her swim in delight. She reached behind and tied the strings on her mask. It completed the ensemble and she radiated elegance, with a hint of seductress all rolled into one.

Caroline's heart still raced as she walked out of the suite door and closed it behind her, with her dress flowing open as she turned towards the elevator to go down to the lobby and into the ballroom. There were other guests milling around, waiting to go down to the lobby for the ball. Caroline had already put her mask on as others were still adjusting theirs. As she took her place in the hallway to go down, she looked around at the others waiting and talking.

Caroline spotted a man at the far end of the hallway who was talking to some other guests; he made her breathe heavily again. His build, his stature, his muscles through the tux… It looked like the same guy from the store! She had to calm down and contain her reactions. She realised that her chest was starting to heave, and she could feel the arousal in her nipples as they made their appearance from under her dress. They were starting to show heavily through the thin fabric and there was no way of concealing them.

She knew there was no calming herself down now as she made her way into the elevator and tried to hide behind other guests to conceal her excitement.

It was too late, however, as others had already noticed, and she was receiving sideways glances from the other passengers. She smiled at them, acting like she had no clue what they were staring at her for. She acknowledged to herself that they most likely were jealous or disapproved of her attire and decided 'to hell with it'. Let them look and think what they like about her.

She was now determined, more than ever, that from that moment on, she wouldn't even try and hide her figure or shorten the length of her strides as this was *her* night, *her* dream, *her* life, and not anyone else's. So, let them look and admire a confident lady. They could stare all they liked. Nothing was going to stop her from enjoying this moment.

She had dreamt of this very day for such a long time; she had pulled out all the stops, and no one's opinion was going to dampen it.

Chapter 2.
The Ball

Caroline arrived in the lobby. She exited the elevator and headed to the ballroom. She noticed, out of the corner of her eye, that heads were starting to turn all around her. Her beauty shone brightly among the guests and she had a host of admirers looking at her flowing gown. She left a trail of comments in her wake as she passed couples, and men alike, on her way to get her pass to go in.

Caroline's thoughts kept drifting and she couldn't help but think back to the guy in the store and the hallway.

'Were they the same guy?? Was he here??' How can she control her reactions through the evening with him jumbling around in her thoughts? The visions of his features swirled around her head as she reached the venue.

The ballroom was mesmerizing; the lights were dimmed to give the setting a sophisticated and refined evening atmosphere. The room had been elegantly adorned with chic decor from top to bottom to add to the masquerade theme.

Veils of sheer fabric hung over the darkened walls added a slight sparkle when the light hit the swaying material just right. Someone had gone to great lengths and depth of detail in creating the perfect setting for the night's festivities. Massive chandeliers hung low from the vaulted ceiling.

The tables were wrapped with a shimmering cloth, the plates, glasses, goblets and silverware were meticulously set on the top at each guest's seat. The centrepiece of each table was a vase with a wide bottom, a slimming middle and a wide opening containing a vast floral bouquet and added a splash of colour to the dark setting. Two miniature masquerade masks, covered in black glitter peeked out from the centre of the arrangements.

More lavish floral pieces decorated the tables around the space, and bottles of spring water were placed all around the room for guests to enjoy as they wandered the floor. The area wasn't just presented well, but the size was just as grand as the fixtures. There were large swathes of fabric flowing down from the ceiling to the walls and cascading down to the floor, making it look like you were inside a huge Bedouin tent, but also bringing the mystical and magical vibe of Paris into the room.

'So sensual.' She thought to herself. It certainly was something to behold and she could have stood there admiring it for hours and still not been able to take it all in. It put her senses into overdrive and made her dreams of what she wanted to do, more of a reality.

She made her way to to the bar, aware that each step displayed her glowing skin through the sensuous slit and turned heads. She felt powerful to be drawing such attention. With head held high, she reached the counter and ordered a glass of wine to calm her nerves.

She felt a surge of confidence course through her veins as she sipped her drink. The mask was working wonders for her self-esteem. She felt unburdened of any worries about people making comments or saying things about her dress, her second skin, as she was now calling it. The fabric was clinging so tightly to her, everyone knew what her body looked like without undressing her. Her thoughts wandered again as she thought about the guy. *'Was he the one from the store?'*

'Was he really here?' The bulging muscles, those shoulders, *'Oh those shoulders and the jeans, well, they didn't leave much to the imagination at all. Now he was wrapped up in a tux.'*

Her imagination ran wild now. *'Oh, what would it feel like to remove the tux and reveal his chiselled muscles and feel them under her fingertips?'* The massive bulge she had seen evoked images she could only dream of. She could envision it taking her to places she had never been before in realities and her fantasies.

'*Stop! Stop!*' She had to control herself. Caroline could feel herself getting so aroused that she knew she was going to have to calm down before she lost complete control too early in the evening. She wouldn't get the chance to enjoy it all if she released too soon.

She swallowed the last of the wine in the glass and ordered another one. She scanned the room, watching the people dancing and arriving to see if she could spot the single men in the room, searching for anyone that kept her gaze. The music that was playing was not what she expected it to be like. It was a mix of moody and sensual music that moved your soul. It penetrated deep inside you and made you feel like you were a part of it. Its rhythm made you drawn to others like going under hypnosis. Not being drawn to just walk to them, and spark up small talk, no, it made you look at others and imagine their lives and what they were doing. It created the desire to get to know them personally.

She could feel the depth of the music deep inside her, riveting her in the emotional depths of the mood being set. She accepted at the first opportunity when she was asked to dance to a slow song. She knew any touch might send her over the edge, but she craved it so badly, she almost couldn't stand it.

The guy looked about her age and maybe a little taller than her in heels and an average build, but it didn't bother her as she needed to feel the warmth of a body next to her right then. She needed the touch, and to feel the music take over her and feel the closeness that only the warmth of two bodies could give.

He pulled her into him and she made sure she was as close as possible so if nothing else came out of this evening, she would have felt a man rubbing against her and would be able to relive it on her own that night in her room. Her thoughts switched to her playing with herself later on in her suite, thinking back to her dances and the guys holding her close and moving against every inch of her body. She became increasingly aroused while she danced.

Caroline felt all she needed, and it worked the way she wanted it to. At the end of the dance, she got a kiss on the cheek and made her way back to her seat at the bar.

She was looking around and then she spotted the guy that she had not been able to keep out of her thoughts in the bath and the store.

'Was it him?' She craned her neck to see further. She was sure it was, due to his size, the tux fitting snugly around his stature, his muscles bugling tightly around his frame.

By now, she didn't care if it was the guy in the store or her thoughts earlier on in the day. She wanted that body; she yearned for it. She watched as he made his way through all of the people and came to the counter. He sat down at the other end of the bar and didn't look as if he was waiting for anyone. Still within her view, his mask shielding his identity just like her mask was doing, she couldn't tell if it was him or not, but she didn't care; she just knew that given the chance she wouldn't be able to resist his advances.

She didn't care about his looks; he could have been twice her age or twice as young, it was her lascivious desire that was driving her.

Caroline knew her heart was racing and that she couldn't control how her body was getting aroused. She had given up trying to keep her emotions and her body in check as her thoughts were now of a more erotic and salacious nature.

Caroline knew what her body desired and craved for but had no idea how to make it happen. She was a CEO, she thrived in the office and business environment, she made pivotal decisions every day, big deals that made her company millions! But in this situation, she was a novice; she wasn't in her element.

To Caroline, it didn't matter that this was not her boardroom, this was *her* time. Why should it only be men that go out and get what they want? It's not a bad thing, it's not wrong. Everyone has their desires, their innermost cravings, and people hide them. They never really live out the things that they want to.

No longer for Caroline; she was going to act on one and live it out in real-time and not hold back. She caught herself thinking again that this was the new improved Caroline, someone that she could be proud of, someone who would hold back no longer and live her life for herself.

She had been sitting at the bar, and guys were coming up consistently and asking her to dance. She was accepting them every time, no matter who they were, just to fulfil her erotic desire.

The fires of lust had been stoked in her body. She knew, with every dance, men had been watching her as her dress flowed and revealed more of her figure.

She had not held back with her movements and wasn't afraid of showing more and more with each dance move she made. The hotter the movements between their bodies got, the more salacious her thoughts were becoming.

Her inhibitions melted away, and with each twirl, she made her dress show off her supple legs. It seemed as though her dance partners were now twirling her with every move, just so they could watch her body on display as she flowed to the rhythm.

The music was driving her passion and she held her body closer and tighter to each guy she danced with. She was enjoying herself but kept an eye on the guy at the bar. With each dance, her body was drawing closer and closer to release and she knew it. The euphoric sensations drove her on to accept every hand offered.

It was a once in a lifetime dream of hers to be at a masked ball and to give in to the temptation of being taken and have someone devour her body like never before. After each dance, she left the guys with a lingering kiss on the cheek, knowing if any of them had gone for her lips she wouldn't have been able to refuse their advances.

She was so close in her thoughts to what she wanted; she knew the slightest touch on her lips would be go-time for the end game. So, she always made the first move for the kiss on the cheek to make sure they knew that's all they were getting… for now. If she had to choose later on, she would, but her desire and cravings were still completely transfixed on her mystery guy at the bar.

Caroline returned from her dance and made her way to the bar and signalled the bartender. He had already seen her heading back towards the bar and walked over and put the wine down for her before she had had the chance to order it. She furrowed her brow and gave a puzzling look. He smiled at her.

"Compliments from the gentleman at the end of the bar," he said, as he pointed to her mystery man. Her heart missed a beat, her stomach fluttered at the thought that her guy had bought it for her and sent it to be ready for when she returned to her seat. He must have been watching her. She flushed inwardly, her body going hot, but she kept her smile steady.

She raised the glass to thank him for the drink, and her hands were shaking. *'Keep control,'* she thought to herself, and as she did, he rose from his seated position and headed toward her.

Her heart skipped a beat again and her body became immediately aroused. Every fibre of her being was so sensitive to the touch. There was no hiding her excitement as her nipples protruded right through her second skin and she wasn't going to hide it. He reached her just as she adjusted the slit in her dress to cover her legs. He looked into her eyes and the feeling was immediate for her. He had those dark, smouldering, brown eyes that you just fell into. They could make you weak at the knee, they could penetrate

you so deeply it felt like he was reading your
thoughts and soul at the same time.

She had to resist letting out her true
desires but couldn't, because it was emanating off
her skin. No words were exchanged; he offered his
hand to dance and she willingly accepted, handing her
glass back to the barman for safekeeping.

He led her to the dance floor; it was crowded
now, but at the same time it seemed empty to her. He
spun her around by her hand over her head and then
pulled her in hard and close to him. That first
thrust against his body sent her over the edge; there
was no fighting it now.

As they danced, her hands ran over his arms and
chest. She couldn't help but pull him in closer so he
would be rubbing hard against her. He was slightly
taller than her but with the heels on, his bulging
tux pants were rubbing her right in the perfect area.
With all the dancing and moving around, the dress was
not covering her at all, and he was positioned

perfectly to hit all the right spots. He was pushing against her without any fabric in the way, and she could tell he was as turned on as she was.

He knew what he was doing; he had had his plan all along. He had seen her from a distance and the red dress was just like sending a red rag to a bull. Once he had got to hold her and dance with her, it wasn't going to change his plan in the slightest. It just made it more vivid in his mind. He had mustered up the courage to approach such a prepossessing lady for the very first time. He had never danced or touched or kissed or been with a lady of her stature before, but seeing her in that dress and as beautiful as she was, the way she gazed at him made him want her more and more.

He wasn't going to be awkward in coming out with it, he was going straight in for the kill. He pulled her closer as the songs changed from one to the next. She felt his powerful arms locked around her and bringing her in even closer as he went in for a kiss, which she didn't refuse. They touched lips for the first time, and she trembled as the first onset of orgasm struck her like a tidal wave. They had been building all day, but she had been fighting them back. Not any longer.

He felt her shudder and kissed her more passionately, his arms wrapped around her holding her tightly to make her feel safe and tamed all at once. Caroline knew it was futile to resist him and she didn't want to at all. She had been thinking about this moment all day; it may not be the same guy from the store, but it didn't matter now.

When they stopped kissing, he nibbled Caroline's lip gently as he pulled away from her, sparking a huge sigh and sharp intake of breath from her. He spun her out from his grasp, but as he did so, his watch caught on the thin strap on her dress and cut it right through. She didn't flinch as it fell off her shoulder. She knew how tight the dress was and that it wasn't going anywhere. But it had just the one strap which connected over her shoulders and around her neck to the other one.

He grabbed the strap and removed it completely from the dress, leaving her breathless once again as he had done on so many occasions already.

He walked her to the back of the room and took her head in his hands and started to kiss her passionately once more. The lights were dimmer in the corners, and no one could see them apart from their shadows. Caroline's hands were all over him; she couldn't stop herself, as they made their way down to the bulge in his trousers and she gasped as the bulge was now bigger and solid. She knew she couldn't and wasn't going to say no.

That was the furthest word from her mind. She wanted to be taken, she wanted to feel those muscles around her, holding her, telling her what to do. She wanted him to be the man that her hands were exploring and feeling all over.

She wanted to be thrown around the bedroom and fucked hard; she wanted it all and more. She undid his zip and reached inside. The thickness was what she felt first.

'That's going to be all mine. Oh my god, take me now, just take me,' she thought to herself as she continued to marvel at his size. He had continued kissing as her hands hit his cock and it made him take a breath to steady himself as she pulled it free from his trousers. He didn't have to think about his next move. He stopped kissing her and looked straight into her eyes. With his palms moving up onto Caroline's shoulders, he smiled and gave a gentle push down. She knew what he wanted, and when his push got harder, she wasn't going to stop him, so she dropped down.

Once on her knees, she was faced with a very thick, massive, rock-solid cock. She didn't hesitate; she knew it was going to be a challenge but one she was more than willing to accept. His head was moist to the touch and very large. As she ran her tongue over it, she realised she had never had a partner so big before. She took a deep breath and had to open her mouth as wide as she could to force him into her mouth.

She couldn't take him all in, he was too big, he was too wide, her teeth gently ran around him as she started going to work on him. She was in a frenzy at this point but she wasn't going to stop for anyone. Her head was going down on him as far as she could and as fast as she could; she wanted to have him lose control like he had made her lose it on the dance floor.

She wanted to taste him as he came in her mouth, but he had other ideas, he was holding back. She felt like she had been down there for ages when he took his hands off her shoulders and lifted her. He slid his hands down and put himself away and she was swimming in his eyes, running her hands all over his arms and chest. He knew he had control. He knew she couldn't resist him. He took her by the hand and went and grabbed their drinks. He looked at her and leaned in, and for the first time that night, he spoke to her in the most sensual voice she'd ever heard.

"You need to finish your wine now, as we are leaving."

She raised her glass to her mouth to meet his demand. She glanced around and all the dance partners that she had been twirling on the floor with looked crestfallen, as they could see they had lost out. None of them averted their eyes from her and they were all still staring hard in her direction.

She looked down and now she could see that her dress had slipped down from when she had been on her knees and was starting to reveal her chest. She went to adjust it and he stopped her.

"No need to worry about it, as you won't be in it for much longer." Caroline looked at him, a wide grin spreading along her lips, and she nodded.

She set her glass down on the bar and he followed suit, took her hand, and they started walking through the crowd to the main entrance of the ballroom. She was cautious as she knew her dress was failing her. He caught her holding it and removed her hands away from it and put his mouth close to her ear.

"Is the dress bothering you that much?"

It was 2:30 am and the place was still busy as could be.

"Yes, it's failing, and it will fall." She glanced around at the crowd.

He took her hand again as they headed towards the doors of the elevator.

"I'll help you out with it."

Her shoes were shining in the lights, and the eyes of the dragon glowed from the lighting of the ballroom. There was about fifteen feet left to go between them and the doors to the elevator at the back of the hotel. They hadn't even made it that far!

Chapter 3.
The Hotel Suite

The guy put his hands around to the back of her dress and unzipped it as her heart raced. He turned her around to face the men she had teased all night before him. He whispered in her ear, sending shockwaves of pleasure through her body.

"All your teasing needs to be paid for. Don't you think it's only fair to them?"

She thought she was wriggling but she wasn't moving at all as he let the dress fall to the floor. The heels and her mask were the only items left on her figure. She was so aroused, her body glowed as she stood there in all her glory. It was such a turn on for her to be free of the shackles that her fantasies had been chained to and inside her for so long. He turned her around; her heart was pounding; her breathing was rapid. They walked to the elevator as the doors opened, and they walked inside. The guys were still watching but had moved closer, wanting to see more.

The doors closed and they were alone. His room was right next to the elevator doors, so he knew when they got there it wasn't going to be long before he had her. He pressed the floor number and they started moving. She wasn't going to wait; his zip was in her fingers as she opened it and pulled him out. She knew this was going to be very tight, but she didn't have a choice now. He lifted her and positioned her above him and slowly lowered her down until the swollen head of his cock was pushing at her slick, moist lips. Her arms were around his neck holding on, but what happened next, she didn't expect.

He smiled at her and released the grip on her waist and dropped her down with desire and passion in his eyes. The sudden drop and the deep thrust inside her made her scream and orgasm at the same time.

She took most of him inside her in an instant. Her legs wrapped around him tightly now to stop her going even further down on him, but he wanted more and put her against the elevator wall and started to thrust deep into her. She lost count of how many orgasms were tearing through her as they were one after the other on the short ride up.

The elevator stopped at his floor and the doors opened. He set her down and grabbed his key card. She knew just one step inside his room, and she wasn't going to be coming out of there the same woman again. Now, she would be the woman she had always wanted to be.

The door to his suite closed behind them as he walked to the bed. He stood at the base of the bed and she walked over, still in the heels and her mask, but she took her time. She slowly started to strip him, removing each layer of clothing with such poise and precision that it was like deconstructing a magnificent work of art. His muscles released from their wraps, she finally got to see his whole torso in its magnificence. His toned and sculptured abs, which were adorned with a sprawling tattoo of a dragon, accentuated his tight muscles.

His chest was covered with tattoos that continued from his arms and flowed on to his well-honed back. As she worked lower, she wondered how on earth she had managed to have him inside her. She discovered that his tree trunks for legs were the reason he was able to support her so easily against the elevator wall.

As he dropped completely free from his covers, she was totally in awe of his physique. She now understood why she had such a desire to be with a man who was built this way.

He grew solid immediately and that's when it hit her; she was going to hurt in the morning. She dropped to her knees again, but this time it was different, there was no hiding, no more slow movements. Caroline was going to take it all in and revel in the moment.

She started sliding her hands along his broad shaft, seeing if it was possible to get him harder or even more engorged. She clamped her hand around his girth and couldn't touch her fingers together; it was certainly a sight to behold. She longed to have him back inside her but also wanted it to last. She could resist no longer.

He wasn't holding back either this time. She took him straight into her mouth, no small bit at a time, and he seemed bigger now. Her mouth stretched at his girth like it hadn't in the ballroom, and she thought back to that moment as she went to work on him. She would have let him take her right there and then in the ballroom if he had tried, she knew it.

His hard, throbbing manhood was the biggest she had ever had. She still couldn't take him all the way in her mouth in the position she was in, so she got up and laid on the bed. Her hand never once released his manhood from her grasp. Head hanging over the edge of the bed, she pulled him towards her mouth with him standing at the base of the bed. She knew he was now in total control but wanted it all.

He moved her hands away from him and placed them at her side. She had already placed him in her mouth, but now he was taking the reins. He positioned his hips so he knew he could get maximum thrust into her and start slowly working his way inside her mouth, thrusting gently to see how much she wanted. As he withdrew, she focused her eyes on his.

"I want it all. I want to try it all. Don't stop."

With those words gently echoing in his head, he took Caroline's lead and started to go further. She knew at some point she wouldn't be able to take any more and her reflexes wouldn't let her, but she was determined to have it all inside her, at least for a few strokes.

He released her hands, but she didn't move them. One hand went to her head to tilt it further back and then he took her other hand and placed it around her own throat. She wondered why but soon found out as the next thrust she felt it in her mouth and throat. Her hand felt his hard cock go down inside as if she was still stroking him.

She thought she must have taken him all until she heard him say "ready?" and then that's when he took her mouth like it was her wet pussy. Long, penetrating, hard strokes, filled her mouth as he bottomed out down her throat.

She gagged but couldn't move, as his frame had pinned her down. She tightened her grip on her own throat, so she could feel every solid inch of him as his balls banged against her face as he started to get more and more aroused. She was squirming with every thrust but loved every moment of it.

He slowed down as her body squirmed more and more, as he wanted her to wait. He withdrew from her mouth, and she inhaled a full breath like she hadn't had any air for a while. Her senses were on overload. He picked her off the bed like she was a feather and turned her around and bent her over the bed. He spread her legs wide and with two towels, he tied her arms to each side of the bed so she couldn't move. He dropped to his knees and without any warning, she felt his tongue slide into her. The reaction was immediate and intense. She didn't hold back her screams of ecstasy as her orgasms were like waves crashing against the shore. They flowed out of her, one right after the other and he didn't stop.

The more she screamed in pleasure, the more he sped up the movement of his tongue inside her and on her clit. He knew exactly what buttons to push in her and he knew he had this one chance to have his dream woman for the first time. He wasn't going to leave a dry sheet in the room.

He continued his explosive work on her now dripping wet pussy for a good while, making her legs buckle on more than one occasion. Her orgasms were more powerful with each passing minute. She couldn't take any more, she wanted him in her, she wanted to be taken. He moved around to untie her, and she refused and just blurted out,

"I want it now!"

He didn't need to be asked twice; the first thrust lifted her off the bed. His giant frame, all 17 stone of pure muscle, had thrust his cock into her. She took it all in that one thrust as she screamed and orgasmed in the split second of him entering her. It wasn't going to be a gentle one, she knew that, but that was just the way she wanted it.

Each thrust was harder than the previous one, each thrust lifting her off the bed, each time he bottomed out inside her. Each time she screamed and moaned, it fuelled the fire inside of him, making him take her harder.

She was making her fantasies a reality now. She was living the deepest, darkest secrets she had kept hidden from her sheltered upbringing, to her modest family life, to her circle of mainly corporate friends, to her social standing back at home. It wasn't like she was told not to date outside her close circle of friends, but they were always trying to set her up with a man that had no adventure in his life. Someone who wanted a cookie-cutter lifestyle. She didn't care now. She would be more than willing to take him home to meet her female friends and say, "Look at this." It would rock their little bubble world.

Her thoughts were running rampant, her orgasms were getting lengthier, and they were starting to join together like they were never going to end. He knew how to make it last. She was starting to lose all aspects of control of her body when he stopped and released her hands.

He picked her up; her legs were like jelly, as if he had fucked the life out of them. He got on the bed and picked her up again and this time lowered her down on him. She was going to make sure this time he exploded inside her. Caroline placed her hands on his chest and started to build a nice slow rhythm on him, sliding up and down.

Taking as many kisses as she could, she wasn't going to take no for an answer from his cock this time. She squeezed herself tightly around him with each movement of her pussy, which was wrapped around his ridged and ribbed cock. His veins were protruding out of him; she knew it would take time, but she knew she could break his resistance.

The longer and more frequently she moved up and down on him, the more he moaned and the more she was matching his pleasure. Had it backfired on her as she was bringing herself off all over again? She knew she couldn't take many more orgasms, as her body was drained. She was so tender to the touch that it was starting to ache, but then she felt the first throb, and she knew she had him.

She quickly sped up. Tightening her lips around him, she started to ride him hard and fast. She felt him start to jerk, his cock seeming to engorge and get wider, and she screamed as he filled her up even more. She was even tighter around him now as she orgasmed harder than she ever had. He was fully engorged when he released a flow of cum deep into her. She had never experienced anything like that.

It was like a cannon had gone off inside her and it was coming straight out of him. Every pulse of cum made him jerk into her and made her feel the delight of his sperm shooting up inside her.

Caroline felt every load he emptied into her. Each time he spasmed, more would shoot out. She knew she was going to be full and dripping when she got off. She could already feel it starting to ooze out of her as she continued to ride him. She wanted to empty him completely and wasn't going to stop until she had accomplished her fantasy.

Caroline was exhausted, and finally, she had it all. She laid beside him as he caught his breath, her hands continuing to wander over his sweat-slicked skin. He was still rock-solid, and she couldn't help but wonder if he could go again right away. He was still having spasms in his body and she wasn't going to waste a drop, so decided to soothe him and take him back in her mouth.

She felt his hands grab her head and hair, then she gasped as he started to take her again while on his back. He started to thrust into her mouth; she was breathing fast through her nose to keep up, and that's when she realised, he had only just started to cum while she was riding him. Once again, he slid into her throat. She gagged hard but was determined not to stop. This moment, for her, may be the only time she got to have body-shattering sex. It was her dream man and when she swallowed all he had to give, he released her head and fell back. She had emptied him.

They laid together for what seemed like hours, breathing heavily and regaining their composure until they finally fell asleep in each other's arms.

She didn't dream that night; she had fulfilled her fantasy and it was better than she imagined it could ever be. All she could think about was what would she fantasize about next. She woke up before him and grabbed the hotel dressing gown and made her exit, though not before she had taken a quick snapshot of the newfound muscles beside her in bed.

'This is going in my journal.'

She left him a note with her number, hoping she could have him again when she returned to England.

Chapter 4.
Enlisting Elizabeth

The plane ride home was just as normal as any flight would be, but the only difference was, she could still feel in her body every heart-stopping pound she had taken the night before, as she ached all over.

She had picked up a leather-bound journal from the outlet stall in the airport and had decided that she was going to keep a record of all her adventures from now on. In the back pages, she was going to detail the twenty-five bucket list fantasies that she would come up with and she made a pact with herself to complete them all. She felt she had to start now, so she began to detail her list of the fantasies to accomplish. The next one would have to expand on her newfound freedom and erotic encounter.

She wasn't going to take any labels or defend her actions to her friends or family; she was living her life for her now. The list wouldn't be in any order of what fantasies needed to come first, but she knew she would complete each and every one she thought of. Her newfound erotic and sexual freedom would serve as a starting point for now, only to be pushed further and further away from what she had already experienced the night before in Paris.

She looked back on that night and thought to herself 'wow I really stood naked in just heels and a mask and didn't care about it'. More than that, it had turned her on. A high-end CEO no one knew, she gave orders to people for a living and there she was, naked, with everyone looking at her and she didn't flinch. She started to get wet all over again, but more than that, she relished it and wanted it more than ever, and wanted more. She thought back to the elevator with the guys staring at her as her guy's hands explored her whole body in front of them as the doors closed.

'Oh, if only,' she thought to herself, *'if only they had got in with them, maybe she would have had them with her, maybe she would have just dropped to her knees and helped them out in the elevator as well, maybe she would have experienced more than one*

guy.' Her thoughts were wide-ranging, but she wrote things down and had every intention of completing each one. Caroline put notes by each one of her fantasies, thoughts on how to complete them or how to go about making them a reality.

Being young at heart and body and in her late 40s, she knew she was in her prime, and she could seduce a guy if needed. The list, as she wrote it down, read:

~Repair guy (break washing machine) open door in just a loose-fitting robe or power dress

~Get invited to a lavish party at an estate or another ball (no mask this time) and go for a much older gentleman or two

~Strip for someone for a night or maybe book herself a gig at a gentleman-only club; preferred event would be a group of normal retired guys in a locked private hall…

The list continued to fill up...

~Get seduced on a beach in broad daylight

~Seduce an intern at work

~Be more submissive to a guy…

'*Can I be more submissive?*' she thought to herself.

~Join a married couple for a night of adventure.

This was the start of something she was going to control.

She knew the next day, at work in her large office in central London, she was going to start planning her year and explore her newfound life, so she picked up her phone and emailed Elizabeth.

I will need you in the office early tomorrow with an iron-clad non-disclosure agreement. Be there at 7 am, two hours before anyone. Get a driver and charge it to me, the agreement is for you.

Caroline said to herself, "Tomorrow is the start of my new hidden chapter, it all begins tomorrow." As she sat back on the plane and closed her eyes, she relived the night before.

She arrived back and got a cab home. She was exhausted and needed some sleep, so as soon as she got in, she changed for bed and crashed out.

Caroline woke up early the following morning, as she wanted to make sure she was in the office before anyone else so that she could have her private meeting with Elizabeth. Caroline and Elizabeth had been friends since they had started at the company many years before. Caroline had always made sure that, with every promotion, she took Elizabeth with her, and they had made it to the top together. Elizabeth was in her mid to late 20s, tall, long-legged with long, flowing blonde hair. She was as gorgeous as Caroline, with a killer body and large perfect breasts. The two women looked great when put together. They worked incredibly well together, and Elizabeth could tell when she needed anything before Caroline even knew. She booked dinners and meetings in advance before Caroline had even called them through; she had booked Caroline's trip to Paris.

Caroline sat her down as soon as she got in and told her everything in detail, reliving every second of her trip. She tried to explain the feeling that she had and how intense and how emotional she had felt. Elizabeth sat and listened to Caroline and took it all in and she kept the feelings that were welling up inside her to herself.

Elizabeth wasn't surprised at all, but couldn't believe the effect it was having on herself.

She had long admired Caroline and now she was in awe of the poise and bravery she was showing within herself; it wasn't just the sexual side of things. She had to try and find a way to keep up her new-found freedom and her status at the company.

They decided that they would work on this together; Elizabeth would help her organize her time away and trips and research things to do. It was a partnership based on friendship and trust that would never break, so she leant forward and signed the document with a smile on her face as she was also secretly hoping that Caroline would take her along for the ride and open her eyes to things. This she thought she would bring up at another time, as she didn't want her to feel she was just following her as she had always done. First of all, they had to get through the day, and then a research dinner for them both in the evening over a bottle of wine.

That evening, they were throwing ideas around about what to do next and what to explore and decided the best course of action was for her to figure out why she was doing this new adventure and what she wanted the result to be. Caroline sat there and thought about it for a minute and said she was tired of the men in her life treating her like she was a trophy and just something pretty on their arms.

She sat there and said,

"All the dates and relationships I have had have all been along the same lines; they just want someone to look nice for them and they were not happy when I spoke my mind and that I normally turned out to be more intelligent than they were."

They wanted to be the alpha male and she was always treated like she didn't exist outside of the relationship and they didn't like her getting involved in the business as much as she was. So, she said,

"I want to take back my life, be the one in control and not have to wait for a partner's permission to say something or do something. I want to be the one in control, but not treat them the way I have been treated." But she wanted to make sure she was in control and turn the tables on the guys in her life, if only for a night or weekend.

They both sat there for the rest of the night, enjoying each other's company and talking about their exes and how they had both been treated, some good, some bad, but it always ended up that they were the ones that we're losing out and Elizabeth could see why Caroline wanted to change things up. It wasn't just sexual, even though Caroline had made it clear that the sex side of it all was going to be amazing, and that for once in her life she would get what she wanted and when she wanted it.

"Women have needs as well," she kept saying and they both agreed that it shouldn't always have to be on the man's terms! If they go out on the prowl, nothing is said apart from a slap on the back and a "*Good on you!*" from all the guys.

Caroline wasn't going to be anyone's notch on the bedpost anymore; she was going to be the one that decided, from here on in, how her sexual appetite was filled and no one else's.

For the next couple of weeks nothing else really changed, Caroline would look at her phone more often, just in case her man from Paris had called her. She wondered if he had even found the number she had left for him, or if he was pissed that she had left him asleep in the bed and not said goodbye.

But she thought *'How many times has a man done that to other women and not looked back…?'* At least she had left him her number and a thank-you note.

She would close her eyes and imagine him walking into her office and her taking control of him and taking him like he had taken her in Paris.

She imagined throwing him on her desk and taking what she wanted from him before kicking him back out of her office the way he had come in, or would she take it slow and keep him at arm's length and tease him till he couldn't take any more? She looked at the pictures she had taken of him lying naked on the bed beside her and still all gloriously hard and ripped and it would send shivers all over her and make her wish she was back in Paris again with him still taking her body to the places he took her that night. She also still smiled to herself that there were over 100 odd people left in the ball when he had made her dress fall off her and they had all seen her body, and she still couldn't believe that she had allowed him to do that to her and how much it still turned her on.

The phone rang and she jumped, but it was Elizabeth was on the other end, telling her that her next meeting was ready and that she was ready to take notes in the interview whenever she was ready. Caroline asked,

"Can you please grab me and you a coffee? I am fighting to keep focused at the moment. Also, can you please order dinner into the office for later this evening?"

Caroline continued her instructions and told Elizabeth, once she was ready and had done that, to bring them in.

Ten minutes passed. The door opened and Elizabeth brought in the coffee and laughed when she handed it to her. Caroline raised an eyebrow at the giggle.

"What's so funny?"

She replied, "You haven't asked me to get you a coffee in the last few years." She continued to explain that she normally went and grabbed them herself and always got her one as well.

Caroline looked at her, smirked and said,

"I am sorry. Yeah, I guess you are right, I'm not the normal boss, am I?" Elizabeth winked and left the room. A couple of minutes later, she brought in the guy for the interview and they sat down and began the process of getting to know each other.

Caroline wasn't the type of person that people normally expected when she interviewed potential employees, as she didn't look at their job life, she wanted to know the person more. Work can be learned by anyone, she always used to say, but family is more important. So the process was always the same and she would always catch them off guard as she would start by reading their resume and then, after a couple of minutes, she would toss it in the bin and say, "Okay, that's enough of that crap! So, who are you and what makes you special?"

Nine times out of ten, they would try and hype back to their work roles and how they would fit in and make a good appointment to the company and those nine out of ten never made it to a second interview. She was always looking for the one person that would be part of her family, be it male or female, they had to fit in, they had to gel with everyone and that took the right kind of person.

This was one of the nine; he kept going on about how he had made his present company even better since he had been there and that he was challenging himself to take a job at her firm. He boasted that he thought he could get to the top faster than most and get even higher than Caroline herself was and that he thought that, as a man, he would be respected more running her division in a few years and grow it more than Caroline had grown it. This wasn't the best way to impress Caroline, and at that moment, Elizabeth closed her pad and stopped taking notes as she knew where it was going and it wasn't going too well for him.

Caroline gave him a hard stare and asked one simple question,

"How would you get to the top of this company in five years?"

His reply shocked even her, as he said, "Well, I would make sure that there were rules in place to make sure everything flowed through me, even on the first day."

His cocky grin continued to spread as he explained that he would make sure what was passed on to Caroline would be taken on by him. He also said something that she didn't like at all, when he stated that no one would get in his way, and if someone tried, he would make sure they weren't with the firm any longer than the following day. He was the one in charge and he would deserve all the credit for getting the jobs through the doors and deals done.

She looked at him with disdain in her eyes and said,

"Well, I can see you're ambitious and I know that you think knocking people out of the way is the best way to do your business, but I will say this. You are not, and will *never* be, a good fit at this firm. There is only room for one boss in my division and I'm it."

Her voice remained firm as she reiterated that the job he was coming in for was an entry position on her floor and that to progress, he needed to realize that anyone on her floor would never act the way he was saying he would be dealing with people. She added that she thought he should stay where he was as he would never make it to the top in a huge firm like hers.

He wasn't happy with her response and said that he would make it one day and that it would be a pleasure to prove her wrong.

This she did like and she smiled as she said,

"When that day comes and you are made a CEO or a partner at a company, I will be the first person on the phone to call you and congratulate you." She stood up to shake his hand and thanked him for coming in.

He shook her hand reluctantly and left with his tail between his legs while Elizabeth stood there speechless. She couldn't believe the arrogance of the guy and followed him out of the room, making sure he went straight to the lift and left her floor.

Elizabeth always called it her floor. Even though Caroline was the CEO, it was Elizabeth who oversaw everyone working on the floor and made sure Caroline was updated on everything that was going on, if someone required help or if she thought something was wrong. Everyone trusted everyone on the floor and there was never any gossip about anybody on the floor. They were all tightly knit together, everyone had everyone's back and that was what made working for Caroline very special indeed. Caroline didn't just like her staff, she loved them completely. That is why Caroline and Elizabeth were so perfect working together; they had introduced this method from the very first day, and it was the only way it was ever going to be.

Elizabeth had been headhunted for years and had always told Caroline when she had been approached and would tell her the same response she had given to them,

"Thank you, but I am happy where I am."

She never once tried to use it to get a raise or bigger perks or bonuses; she stayed because she loved her job and Caroline.

Chapter 5.
Scotland

Caroline wanted to get away on her own and seclude herself away from everyone so she could think long and hard about what she desired most. Elizabeth knew Caroline did her best thinking when alone and away from the office and home. She had a meeting in Scotland scheduled for the following week, so that's when they decided she should make her short escape and take her journal with her to write down some ideas.

Caroline liked to explore, so they found a small island off the coast of Scotland where there was a restored old castle. It had been donated by the old owners who had passed away and had been looked after by a trust for years. But as far as they could tell, the place was closed for the season and only available for private bookings, so they called around and, as luck would have it, no one was in it or had booked it.

The castle was stunning; it had been restored to its former glory and every detail that they could research and either find or make had been taken care of, down to the finest detail. It had a clear, spring-water loch in the grounds and looked perfect. They booked a small seaplane to get Caroline there and pick her up. The weather looked like it would be free and clear of any storms, so she would take some relaxing clothes as well as some warm ones, just in case.

She flew to Scotland for her meeting and all went well. They finished early in the day, so she spent the rest of the day getting essentials that she needed for her trip. She called ahead to the booking office to ask them if it was possible for her to book in early. She arrived at the small country airport in plenty of time and the pilot was there waiting for her. Caroline introduced herself and so did her pilot. She smiled at him and gazed over him thoroughly. She guessed he looked in his late 50s but looked amazing for his age.

He was full of knowledge about the isle and said she would love it as a retreat. They got to talking and he had been flying to the isle for over 50 years. She inquired about his age and he said he would be 68 the following day. She was shocked and told him what age she had thought he was when she had first seen him.

He let out a hearty chuckle and said,

"Well, that's a compliment I will gladly take, and if that's the case, there's still a chance for the old guy yet, then."

They both laughed and she made a quick comeback, and stated,

"I have dated men that look older than you, so more than a chance." She rubbed his leg and winked.

She caught herself doing it and stopped, as she didn't want to give him a heart attack while he was flying her to the island. She let out a small giggle;

"You are older than my dad." She continued to laugh at him.

With a broad grin, he replied,

"There is plenty of life left in this old guy! And you, Miss, have made my day."

The castle was on a small island and situated in the southern part overlooking the bay and the loch. It was built on the highest part, about half a mile from the dock, and had been designed to defend the Scottish mainland during the wars. He told her the history of the island and the folk tales about the castle and the old owners.

The castle had been in their family for generations, till the last one had passed away. He also told her tales of the lords of the castle back in the day, taking their rights to any female that entered the castle grounds. He joked that since he was still in with a chance, he may take up that right with her.

Caroline laughed, "If only you were at the castle, I wouldn't have had the right to refuse you and would have accepted gladly and willingly."

The story intrigued Caroline and got her worked up, thinking that if she had been around then, would they have taken her too?

They talked about travel and where she had been and if he travelled. She found out he hadn't left Scotland in his life, as at an early age, he had taken over his dad's business of ferrying people to and from all the islands to the mainland. His dad had taught him to fly when he was young and he had got his pilot's license on his 16th birthday and then commercial when he was 21. She made a point to him that he needed to visit London as it was her birthday in a few months and she would return the kindness he had shown her. He smiled and said that would be wonderful and thanked her.

She got on the phone to Elizabeth to organize dinner, travel and a hotel for him at her expense and invited Elizabeth to join them as their birthdays were only a week apart. She accepted and said she would book things right away, Caroline said she would explain everything when she returned.

He flew her over the island a few times so she could get the lay of the land. He landed the plane safely about half a mile from the castle. He told her the keys were always left under the rocks by the main door of the castle so she would be able to get in. He knew this as he was the one that had delivered supplies to the castle when it was being used.

He gave her his number just in case the weather closed in and said to call him and he would come out on a boat to get her. She was grateful for his kindness.

'Such a nice gentleman,' she thought to herself, *'Flirty and a teasing old man, but very kind.'* He carried her belongings ashore and bid her farewell. On walking away, he joked that she should be on the lookout for the hooded watchman.

"He has been alone for centuries and has had no female company." He winked at her.

She laughed at him and said,

"If he is that old, then he can have whatever he wants!"

With that, the pilot chuckled and went back to his plane, waved and said,

"Don't say I didn't warn you!" roaring with laughter as he went.

She started walking away and stopped and called out to him,

"Wait!" Caroline ran up and gave him a big kiss on the cheek and wished him a happy birthday for the following day.

He stopped in his tracks.

"That's not any way to kiss a gentleman on his birthday." Caroline was taken aback as he said it in such a stern, powerful voice. She was startled till he grabbed her and planted one right back on her lips that was just as passionate, long and lingering as the ones she had had in Paris. She didn't stop him at all and kept it up for him for his birthday and for how nice he had been to her. Plus, *'Oh my…'* she liked it, it was strong, yet tender and passionate, but also, with a hint of being taken. A minute or two passed and he stopped.

She caught her breath,

"Wow… If that's the kisses you give, I want another one on my birthday and more." She laughed and started the short walk to the castle as he waved, got back on the plane, started it up and moved away.

She turned and walked toward the castle. Looking back, he had already taken off and was flying into the distance. She thought back to their conversation and thought to herself,

'Did I really just say if you had been at the castle, I wouldn't have had the right to say no?' She laughed to herself at the thought of getting it on with a guy over thirty years older than her. *'What was she thinking?'* She giggled again. But then, nothing surprised her anymore about her thoughts and

she knew that given the chance, and her thoughts, she would have graciously accepted and let him have her.

It was then that she realised she had said she wanted more on her birthday and that she had already invited him and had had Elizabeth book his tickets and set it up. She laughed to herself loudly; at least Elizabeth would be there to keep an eye on things.

She reached the castle in the mid-afternoon. It was stunning, with walls covered in ivy on the outside of the gates and once inside the gates, it was as if it was just as it had been back years before. The walls were made of massive stone blocks, turrets for defence, with tall towers that looked right out of a movie set. It was breath-taking. Caroline walked towards the big doors at the front of the castle and noted that the old guy was right, the keys were there. *'Note to self,'* she thought, *'give him a huge hug and kiss when he picks me up in three days.'*

She let herself in and closed the door, which sounded like they do in every movie, a loud creaking sound as the oak door swung open, and then a thundering bang when closed and locked. It was an out-swinging, solid, heavy wooden door on old forged hinges.

She put her cases down and followed the guy's instructions to where the passage was to the generator that the trust had installed. It started the first time; she checked the fuel gauge and it was full, so no need to refill it. The lights flickered on around the castle, and it looked magnificent in the candle-style lights that had been fitted. She felt like the lady of the castle, but then she thought she would rather have been a single female that had wandered into the grounds like the old guy had said, and then she would have been taken. She smiled and joked about it in her head. She made her way upstairs to one of the ten grand bedrooms; the beds had been wrapped in plastic to keep the embroidered fabric spotlessly clean. She chose the grandest room and removed the covering.

The dust had not gotten onto the sheets and they were as clean as if they had just been washed. She looked down and realised she had been so lucky as her jeans and shirt and hands were covered in dust. She knew her face must be as well.

'*Loch time.*' she thought. She stripped off and put on the swimsuit she had brought with her for such a swim. She found her way out of the castle and followed the small path down to the loch. It was crystal-clear blue, like something she had seen in National Geographic, and she felt so at peace there.

Caroline got to the water's edge and jumped right into the cool water, rinsed off and returned to the shore. She sat and ate some of the food she'd had prepared for her at the hotel in Scotland. She opened a bottle of wine and just sat looking at the loch and scenery. On finishing, she didn't waste any time, but got ready and jumped in again. It was cool but not cold, and it made her nipples stand right out.

The water felt so nice against her skin and she washed off any of the dust that she had missed before. Looking around, she could see for miles, hills on one side and the sloping valleys tailing off down towards where they had landed. She couldn't see the sea as she was on the castle side of the island, but the sun was out, it was peaceful and quiet. She was alone with her thoughts.

Caroline decided to make a list in her head of things she would like to do for her bucket list and then transfer them to the back of her journal. She looked at the castle and thought,

'*Bring a guy here and let him seduce me.*' That was a thought that would be magical. She played it through in her mind, what she would wear, would he ask, or just take what he wanted? Would it be once or over and over? Would it last minutes or hours or days? Would she be tied up or free to play?

Would he be rough or gentle, would he be young or old, or would there be more than one? Her hands were wandering all over herself and before she knew it, she had taken off the top and bottoms and was as naked as the day she was born. She didn't care; she was alone and even if she wasn't, she had been stripped two weeks earlier in front of hundreds of people and fucked beyond what she had been used to. Nothing worried her now, she had been set free. The evening was closing in, so she decided to call it a night, so she picked up her bikini and headed back to the castle. Pointless getting dressed. Who was she going to scare, the birds?

Caroline arrived back at the castle and went back inside. Turning around, she closed the doors with their usual old-sounding loud creaking and bang that echoed when they closed. She locked the doors and headed upstairs; she had been on the go all day and needed rest. It didn't take long before she was on the bed laying there with just her thoughts to herself, the thoughts about the journal and the bucket list.

Was it okay for her to do this? It was, at least under her terms, her rules and her choices, it wasn't like she was going out every night and getting another man, it was a list of fantasies to complete. If she had been a guy, she would have had high fives and a million hits on social media by now. But she was a woman, a CEO of a huge company, and a lady.

She had the right to do what she wanted to do, and no one could stop her. She smiled to herself and thought, *'I am doing it.'* With that, she laid back down and was ready to dream. Would it be Paris or something else? It didn't take long before she was asleep.

Caroline woke up later than usual but was so relaxed and rested. She walked to the window and looked out; it was a glorious sunny day already, no need for warm clothes, this was time for a nice summer dress. She sat down and ate breakfast and made her way outside with her journal in hand, walked the shore, and she sat down on the sand. She thought the first thing to add would be her next adventure:

~show my pilot around London on my birthday, followed by a nice dinner with him and Elizabeth at her apartment, and in brackets (get my birthday kiss from him if not two or three) but then a thought crossed her mind.

Elizabeth… a way to keep her secret from getting out. If she had thought her pilot was no older than 50, maybe Elizabeth would as well. She hatched a plan in her head to have a really good birthday dinner at hers. She lay back and thought about how she could make it happen, and what Elizabeth would do. 'Yes,' she thought, '*the birthday kisses would be for Elizabeth, not me.*' She would have one, but who would want to miss one of his kisses? She knew that Elizabeth couldn't after she had had one and wouldn't want to either. She laid down by the edge of the water for hours with plans going through her head and decided that she would just let it take its course but with a little push from her. Caroline got out her phone and sent Elizabeth a text to make sure she had planned dinner at her house and that she would be there. She told her not to invite anyone else, as she wanted it to be a thank-you dinner as well as their birthday celebration.

Elizabeth replied that she wouldn't invite anyone else and was it okay if she stayed over as well, so she could drink and would get a taxi to Caroline's in the afternoon? She completely understood that it would be just the three of them ... and said she would not listen to them getting up to anything but said she couldn't promise as she might have to.

Caroline laughed to herself and thought, *'Little does she know that the noises will be from Elizabeth, not me.'* She grinned about plans in place and the bait already taken. So, she decided not to worry about that anymore as it was already sorted and in the works. She just stayed on her back, looking up at the pure blue sky in the most tranquil of places.

She looked at the weather forecast and saw perfect weather ahead for her whole stay. The evening looked nice and warm as well. She decided to have a night picnic, go skinny dipping and lie out, naked, under the stars. So, she went back to the castle and picked up some food she had brought with her and took some blankets and a towel back down to the loch. She laid them out beside a sandy area and in the ground, she stuck some candles she had found in the castle. Plan set and food ready, '*Now time for a swim,*' she thought to herself. She slowly stripped off and admired the view, standing up taking in the scenery, feeling the clean air all over her perfect body. She loved it and walked into the loch; the water felt wonderful again. Her skin had been warmed by the sun as she just laid back and floated on the surface. She thought to herself, '*What a place to have fun and no one around to take advantage of it. Hmmm... I have the pilot's number,'* but she wanted to save him for another time. So, she just shouted out loud

"No one can see me skinny-dipping! It's such a shame!" She burst out into fits of laughter.

The time flew by as she sat beside the loch writing down things to do in her journal. The list was getting long but she had done it this way so she could sit back at a later date and filter out the ones that didn't fit with what she wanted to do.

That night, she slept under the stars and was so content. She realised that all the stress she had at work had all been washed away by the isle and her wish list and Paris. *'This is what I am supposed to do,'* she thought to herself, *'run a company and have fun!'* She knew she would be happier at work and also her staff (family she called the ones directly under her) would reap the rewards of her newfound relaxed mode.

She slept so soundly that night, which was good, as the next day she would be leaving and heading home. The following morning, she awoke with a start as she heard the plane flying in. It was the first time in what she thought was forever that she had slept in. It was past midday and he had landed to pick her up. She panicked as she thought she didn't want to keep him waiting. So, she grabbed her blankets and her stuff and just walked as fast as she could go back to the castle. She got to the castle before he got there, put the stuff down by the door and then realising she was naked, she laughed and shouted,

"I'm still naked, and no one can see!" When she stopped, she realised she wasn't alone anymore as he must have heard her, *'Teasing time,'* she thought with a smirk. She waited by the door for him to walk up the hill and fumbled around with the key, trying to look as if she couldn't get it in the lock.

He rounded the corner of the track and she turned around to face him.

"It's stuck, I can't get back in." He looked at her, "I don't think anyone has used that pickup line ever before on me." He laughed as he walked over and took the key and put it in and unlocked the door and walked into the castle in front of her.

She batted her lashes at him and teased, "Oh! My hero!"

He looked at her, sternly, as she was about to enter the castle. "My dear, I've come to collect."

"I will be packed in five minutes. I am so sorry." Thinking he was upset, she started to rush to get her belongings.

"No, my dear. Remember when you said, 'if you were in the castle before I walked in, I wouldn't be able to say no?' I've come to collect."

She looked at him in shock.

"You dirty old man!" She threw her head back and laughed, but as she looked at him, she could tell he wasn't joking. As he unzipped his trousers, she took a deep breath and thought, *'Well, this isn't what I planned for him…'* She stood and watched as put his hands into his trousers, looking like he was about to remove himself. She thought again, *'He isn't joking!'* and went to bend forward and get on her knees ready to accept it willingly into her mouth. He just stood there and laughed.

"I am only joking, my dear. I just wanted to have you naked a little bit longer and tease you." His smile was broad.

She got up and playfully beat him. "You had me going and I was going to take it! You just wait, there goes your tip."

They went upstairs, packed away her clothes and she got dressed and recovered the bed like it was as if no one had been there. They left the castle, locked up and placed the key back where she had picked it up from.

She looked back at the building as they started to take off, saying,

"One day I'm coming back and getting laid in that castle."

He joked, "I can land again if you want to do it now." They shared more laughter as he flew off toward the mainland. She turned to him, placed her hand on his leg and rubbed it.

"You had the chance; I would have willingly had you take me back there." She slid her hand onto his crotch. "You wouldn't have had an issue getting up now, would you?" She watched as he grew. She looked up at him, "Plenty of time, you're coming to London in 6 weeks - you'll get laid then." Little did he know he would be having Elizabeth, not her.

Caroline smiled as they just talked and chatted all the way back. On landing, he carried her stuff to her waiting car, and she gave him a warm hug.

"Don't forget, 6 weeks, all your travel is taken care of. So just be there and I will pick you up at the airport."

He nodded, "I wouldn't miss it for the world."

She got in and her driver took her back to London. The next couple of weeks were busy for her, with new deals to be done, meetings, quick trips and meeting with Sarah in secret to cement plans on what she wanted to do and accomplish in her new role.

She was determined that this was for her, not just her… It was for all women to prove that men don't have the upper hand.

It would show that women too can take the lead and have fun without having the bad labels thrown at them, and no high fives except from Elizabeth. She would go out to dinner with friends and drinks with Elizabeth and have random men ask her if she wanted a drink. She would look them up and down and just fire back with her newfound confidence, *"How many notches would there be on your bed if you managed to have me?"* She just wanted to throw it back at them; she wasn't doing it to embarrass them, just to make sure they knew she wasn't for taking on their terms.

Chapter 6.
The Art of the Deal

Caroline spent most of the next day in her office, sorting out paperwork and having meetings with her colleagues about upcoming deals or events that they had to plan to entice companies to let them represent them or sell to them. She faced men older and younger than herself and mostly the younger ones were the hungrier of the groups. They seemed to think, when they entered the office or boardrooms for the meeting, that as soon as they saw her sitting there looking as gorgeous as she did, that she was there for show and not to give them any hassle getting in their way.

Little did they know that she was doing it to lure them in, knowing that as soon as they had had their say, she would counter and then they would know they were not dealing with just a gorgeous lady behind the table, but a formidable businesswoman who could, and would, bend them around to her way. More often than not, she would get her way, and the times that she didn't get it all her way and they wouldn't accept she knew what she was talking about and stick to what they wanted, it was those times she enjoyed the most as she would put the deal on the table and say, "One-time offer. If you don't accept, it won't be as good a deal for you next time".

These meetings would be the ones that she loved as she knew she would get up and leave five minutes after putting the offer down on the table and walk out. These were the ones that she would make the most out of for her company, as she knew they wanted to deal but were not seeing it her way at all.

They needed time to restructure it in their favour and she wouldn't take that. She always worked it in favour of the business deal she was working on, not only for the shareholders of the firm she worked for, but also for the employees of the firms she was doing business with. She had made it to the top of her firm not just because she was ruthless in her determination to get there, but because she looked after everyone.

She always structured all her deals to make sure that the people at the lowest end of the pile got their share of the deal as well. That's where she had started and she made sure that she always gave back. That's why she had kept Elizabeth with her all the way up; she had confided in her about how she wanted to run things and make sure even the cleaners at her firm were on a good deal. She respected everyone working for her firm, no matter what job they did.

Caroline looked at it as a family, and families rise and fall together. When one does well, they all do well, and each and every employee at her firm had the chance to buy shares in the company, and however many they bought with each paycheck, she made sure the firm would match it for the employees. As a result, she was loved for it by everyone in the firm. Even the board of directors loved her for doing it, as everyone in the firm pulled together as one.

The HR department hadn't had a complaint from anyone since Caroline had made the changes and put her plan into motion and had been in charge. All they dealt with was the mundane things in a company, like helping set up dividend accounts and dealing with outside efforts to destabilize their employees, such as other companies trying to poach their staff members.

Other companies wouldn't realize this until they were in business with them and then it would be made abundantly clear that they did it her way or there was no deal to be made. But once they were on board and they realised the effect it would have on their own employees, they never looked back and always enjoyed a fruitful and special relationship with Caroline.

Caroline would rather walk away from a deal than get into business with a company that did not treat their staff the same way that she would treat her own staff. Even though her firm had over 300 staff members, from cleaners, to heads of departments, to managers, she knew when each and every birthday was and had them on her calendar. Once a birthday was approaching, she would email their department head two days before, and they had to make sure that there was either a cake or a special lunch organized for that team for the day, or a gift sent out from the firm. No one was ever forgotten, she always made sure of it.

It was on one of those occasions in a boardroom at a firm that they were trying to do a deal with, that they would learn that she wasn't to be messed with and that she knew what she was doing and that her way of running things would be the best way for them to grow their company. They wanted their investment to grow bigger and she had agreed to a sit-down meeting with them to discuss what they wanted, and for her to tell them what she could do to help grow their company, in the best interests of her firm as the investor and for them as a company.

She had travelled with her team of two advisors and Elizabeth to the company and was shown to the boardroom to wait for the board members to join them.

This was at 11 o'clock in the morning; by 11:45 they were still waiting, so Caroline decided that this wasn't for her and got up to leave. At that moment, two guys walked in and introduced themselves and said they were sorry for being late. They added that the rest were on the way and would be with them shortly.

Elizabeth leaned forward and reminded Caroline that the guy that she had just spoken too was the guy that had come for and an interview with her for a job and she had turned him down. She showed her the notes on her laptop of the interview to refresh her memory and after reading them, Caroline knew who he was right away.

The rest of the board members came in to join them and they all sat down again, ready to discuss their proposed multi-million-pound investment and what they were willing to give to Caroline's company in return for the investment.

Caroline sat back and enjoyed listening to them, as most of what they were saying sounded good on paper, but she wasn't interested in what facts and figures they had written down. She was still furious inside for being kept waiting and wanted to know the real reason why.

They were not willing at first to tell her, until Caroline looked at her group and said;

"I guess it is time to leave. Or, would you like me to tell you why you were late myself?"

They looked at her like she was joking about leaving, until she stood up to make her exit. The gentleman in charge of the board members spoke to her.

"Hold on, please, tell us, then, why we were so late getting into our meeting with you."

Caroline glared at him.

"That is an easy one for me to explain. You see that gentleman at the back?" She pointed to the guy that had been to an interview at her firm. "He persuaded you to make a show of strength towards us so that we knew that you were in charge. He told you that you should be late for the meeting and keep us waiting so that it showed that you were in control, and not us." She continued to stare down each man. "How do I know this? He came for an interview with us and told me what he thought was the best way to do business and that he would have my job within a couple of years."

The CEO of the company looked over his shoulder at his staff member and then back at Caroline. "Okay, you have it right so far, please continue."

"You see, his idea of keeping a company in control is to step over everyone on his way to the top and then to scare them into being loyal to him and to take all their hard work as credit for himself. We parted ways not even five minutes into the interview because I wouldn't employ someone with that business mentality." Her eyes and firm words pierced every person in the room. "I stopped the interview. I do not know what position he holds at your company and I don't care. All I know is, if you have him and take his opinions on how to treat people and his way of making people feel inferior to him as your business ethic, then I am sorry, we won't be investing in your company." With that final comment, she stood up to leave.

The guy who had had the interview stood up and laughed at her. His words dripped with condescension.

"You see, I am a board member of the company now, so I think you owe me an apology. Oh, *and* a congratulations, like you said you would give me if I made it to the top."

The chairman of the board turned to him, his fury present in his expression. "Yes, you are on the board of directors, but all of the directors are here right now, and you never told us you went for an interview at another firm either. We voted you onto the board and we can vote you off. I would sit down, if I were you, before we move to a vote right now."

Caroline thanked the board members for their time and got her team together and left the meeting. A few weeks later, she received notice that the company was heading for administration and that they had parted ways with the guy who interviewed with her. She set up a meeting the following day to see if she could help turn around the company and save the jobs of the workers. She didn't have an issue with the company, it was a sound investment for her firm. She knew if she explained to them what to do and installed someone in the company of her choosing from her firm, that there would be a serious monetary investment for her firm that would not only save their company, but also their company's employees.

She had a soft spot for staff members but was a very good business lady as well, and she knew that if she turned it around, their investment would be worth ten times more in a couple of years and would benefit both parties.

Chapter 7.
Joint Birthday

Caroline always knew what to do in business and had Elizabeth with her in all her meetings. Her personal goals had changed but she still confided in Elizabeth, keeping everything that was discussed completely between them. She trusted her completely and wouldn't do anything at all unless they had discussed it, just as she did with her business. Some things were kept from her, though, not to hide it from her, but to wait till the right moment to share.

She would sit with Elizabeth for hours, figuring out plans for her to-do list and one that always came to mind was being a stripper (she had no idea why) miles away from the humdrum of London and miles from her corporate friends. She also had the fantasy of joining a couple or even being with a younger guy.

She decided one of those was next, but it was her and Elizabeth's birthday soon, so she didn't want to make any plans until after that. Her pilot friend, saviour, and total dirty old man arrived on Friday, and Caroline and Elizabeth picked him up at the airport. When he saw them, he joked about what he had done to deserve being picked up by two beautiful women and that one on each arm would do nicely.

They all laughed and obliged, taking his arm and walking side by side. Caroline thought he must have felt like a millionaire or royalty with a lady on each arm. The driver opened the door for them, and they got into the car and he sat in the back beside Elizabeth. They headed to the hotel they had booked for him, which was right around the corner from Caroline's place.

On the drive back, they were talking about Caroline's trip to Scotland and he turned toward Elizabeth and, not in a hushed voice, said,

"Elizabeth, it was nice of you to come and pick me up and at least Caroline is dressed this time."

She hadn't told her about that part as she wanted to keep it a secret so her plan would go without a hitch. Elizabeth turned to face them both and grinned.

"Tell me more."

He continued with the story that he teased her, and she was about to run. Caroline stopped him, "Honey, there would have been no running at all. I was willing to accept and take what you could give out of those old bones. But as I recollect, you were the one that stopped, not me." Her smile was mischievous.

Elizabeth turned to him. "Yep, that's right, she doesn't turn and run from anything. I'm starting to think she has the right attitude and I'm following suit."

Caroline looked at her in shock and thought to herself, *'This is going to be easier than I anticipated.'*

They dropped the pilot off and arranged what time they would come and escort him to dinner. They would let him go and relax after his flight and so they left him with the receptionist at the hotel.

They got back to the car and Elizabeth turned to Caroline. "You kept that one quiet, you little devil." Caroline chuckled at Elizabeth. "He owes me a kiss tonight, and you as well, since it's our birthdays. Okay, right now, it's time for shopping. I'm treating you to a new dress and shoes for your birthday and dinner tonight."

Neither needed to be asked twice for dress and shoe shopping.

Elizabeth turned to her boss and friend. "Thank you. Let's tease him tonight then, and get dresses that reveal our curvy features, and shoes that are high to show him if he was a lot younger, what he would have been able to pull."

Caroline smiled to herself and thought *'He will pull tonight without a doubt.'*

They both agreed to head straight for Oxford Street, parked and went on the hunt for something that would be so irresistible he would want them both.

Elizabeth was looking at long dresses until she found a stunning dress with a cut out at the cleavage, no back, and sides which were cut right around the sides of her chest. It would leave nothing to the imagination, and it was so figure-hugging it would drive the pilot wild. She looked at Caroline.

"What do you think?" She held the dress close to her body, admiring the fabric.

Caroline replied "I thought you said tease, not give him a heart attack! Don't forget the shoes, though."

Caroline picked a longer dress in a stunning light sea-blue shade that showcased her long legs and had two slits on either side. The slits went up so high that when she walked, both her legs were on display all the way up her thighs. The dress was backless and had a plunging neckline, showing off the most sensuous cleavage that any guy would want to see.

They went and picked out matching shoes with pointed toes, and 4-inch stiletto heels. They smiled at each other and headed back to the car to go back to Caroline's penthouse apartment and get ready for dinner.

Elizabeth had taken care of dinner and was having it delivered to the apartment in the evening, ready for their guest arriving.

Starter

Smoked salmon with prawns, horseradish cream & lime vinaigrette

Main course

Honey-glazed spiced roast goose & confit potatoes

Dessert

Lavender poached pear with Poire Williams pudding

She had already had a dozen bottles of hand-selected wine delivered the day before to have them chilling ready for dinner. As usual, Elizabeth had not left anything to chance and had made sure she had all of her bases covered to make sure the evening went without a hitch.

They sent the company driver to collect their gentleman friend so that they would have extra time to make sure everything was ready and perfect for their joint birthday dinner. Caroline was dropping hints all the time about the pilot and how nice and pleasant he was.

She kept dropping little tidbits here and there to make sure he kept in Elizabeth's head. She wasn't leaving anything to chance.

Their guest for dinner arrived and they went to greet him. Both were now dressed to perfection in the outfits that they had bought earlier, and they looked gorgeous with both having had their hair done and now in just the dresses, heels and nothing more.

Caroline was going to make this a night to remember and also make sure to stick to her plan of not having her secret slip out. Their pilot was now standing at the door and looking at these two sensual ladies that he was about to have dinner with. He took in the sights of their beautiful bodies that were on show through their curve-hugging dresses.

He had already seen what Caroline's looked like at the castle and his eyes were drawn to Elizabeth. She was the one that was standing looking just amazing and he hadn't seen what she was hiding under the dress yet. But with what she was wearing, it didn't take much thought to know it was toned and young and trimmed, as the dress fitted so nicely to her curves that his eyes must have been bulging out of his sockets while looking at her.

They invited him in, and both gave him a hug and a kiss on the cheek to welcome him. He took the glass of wine that they offered to him.

"This is my first ever visit to London."

They sat around talking for a bit and then, when dinner was ready, they sat down to the mouth-watering meal that Elizabeth had ordered. They talked like they had known each other for years.

Caroline was always dropping hints about the trip to the island and how it felt to be naked and free, lying next to the loch and how tranquil the whole island and visit had been. She also made sure she brought up the fact of him catching her naked at the front of the castle, just to gauge his reactions.

After dinner, they went to the living room which had an amazing balcony leading off it so that you could see the whole of the London skyline at night. With it being the penthouse, they had no one overlooking them and it was time to put her plan into motion. She stood on the balcony with Elizabeth and her pilot, and turning toward him, she refreshed his memory that he owed her a long sensual kiss for her birthday and not to forget that it was a joint birthday party and Elizabeth was owed one as well.

She set out the rules that Elizabeth and her kisses had to be extremely sensual and he had to kiss them both like they were his and that he was to play it as if he was seducing them. Elizabeth looked at Caroline.

"I didn't agree to a kiss like that. But it's my birthday next week, so you go first, and I'll go next."

Their pilot didn't have to wait long before Caroline walked right up to him.

"Okay then, let's go. Where is my kiss?" Her lips curved into a devilish smile.

A red-blooded male standing in front of two gorgeous ladies, he wasn't about to turn it down and without any more direction, he started to kiss her gently but also passionately. Taking his time to explore her lips and neck he wanted to find out all of the tender areas around her head that would send her over the edge, plus making sure all the time that he was looking at Elizabeth to let her know she was next.

Caroline already knew what to expect and whispered to him while he was kissing her neck that she wanted him to really, really seduce Elizabeth for her. He went in for the big kiss, locking lips with her and sending waves of ecstasy through Caroline's body. She pulled him in closer and took her time enjoying it.

He slowly released her and ended the kiss, so she stepped back and took it all in. "Wow, now that was a kiss." Her body shivered with pleasure as she looked at Elizabeth. Caroline walked up to her and whispered in her ear that he was hard as a rock and that he was primed for the taking, and that she should take full advantage of it.

Elizabeth grinned at her.

"Let's see how he kisses a younger woman first, then we will see."

He heard Elizabeth say this and went up to her. On reaching her, he walked around her slowly and using just the tips of his fingers, he caressed her body very gently, making sure to send goosebumps all over her body. He stopped behind her and moved her hair away from her neck and slowly kissed the outline of it very gently. While doing this, he looked around and spotted that there was a big soft rug on the floor laying in front of the fireplace and thought, 'this may come in handy in a few minutes.'

He continued to kiss her neck and made his way around to stand in front of her. Taking his hand, he placed it around her waist and slowly let it slip down to her tight, firm butt, gently squeezing it. He then leaned in and started kissing her taking the time to make sure her lips trembled under his touch. He then proceeded to explore her mouth tenderly with his tongue.

She expected him to keep kissing more but he stopped and took her breath straight away by swooping her up in his arms and carrying her over and laying her down on the rug. As he laid her down, he started to slowly slide his hands down her body while releasing her and immediately kissed her neck which made her sigh.

He went on to kiss her neck and lips so gently and sensually that she was starting to run her hands over his body without knowing she was doing it. By this time, he had gone in for her welcoming mouth and laid a full, hard, passionate kiss on her and she just threw her arms around him and brought him in tightly while he edged his body gently on top of her and in between her legs, spreading them wider so that he would have full access to them when the time came.

He became more passionate in his kissing, exploring the deepest realms of her mouth with his tongue and sending her even closer to wanting more. He didn't want to bring her to that just yet, so he stopped kissing her and slowly made his way down to her now heavily breathing chest. Using both hands, he started to caress each breast gently while still sliding the tip of his tongue down her neck toward her ample breasts, making sure that he didn't go to fast as he wanted this to last for as long as he could before he wanted her as well and wouldn't be able to take any more. After a few minutes, he went back to kissing her and then stopped and looked at her.

"Happy birthday! How was your kiss then?"

She looked at him and didn't say another word, as she put her hand around the back of his head and pulled him in for another one. This time, she took control; while he was kissing her, she placed both her hands on his shoulders and started to push him down toward her now soaking wet pussy and it didn't take long before he realised what she wanted.

Caroline noticed she was taking control, and this was on her terms and not his. Once he was there, her hands stayed on his head and she pushed him hard on her to make sure she had the pressure that she wanted and was getting most importantly what she craved for. She had been hearing all about Caroline's adventures and this time, she wanted to start her own.

He didn't mind her holding his head down there as he certainly wasn't going to say no to having such a young lady for the evening, and it was more than likely a once in a lifetime chance. So, if she wanted to be in control, he wasn't going to say no.

Caroline was sitting on the sofa watching all of this happen and smiling to herself, knowing her secret life was now completely safe as there was no way Elizabeth would ever let it slip now, knowing what was about to happen. She smiled and enjoyed the view, now she had the chance to watch Elizabeth and admire her body. She thought to herself, *'I am going to have to put her on my bucket list but will have to play it very carefully.'*

Elizabeth was now at the point of no return; Caroline's pilot friend had taken his cues from her and was exploring every single inch of her glorious pussy and was enjoying every second of it. She tasted so sweet to him and he couldn't get enough of all of her gorgeous, flowing juices, but Elizabeth now wanted more and released his head from her grasp.

She let him get up and moved to stand up and once on her feet, she let her dress fall to the floor and told him to strip as she wanted him now. He obliged and didn't waste any time getting out of his suit and being ready to take her. He was already as hard as he could be and primed, ready to take her. He was going in for a kiss before they laid back down, but she stopped him.

"All in good time. You'll have to wait." With that, she took his tie off the floor and blindfolded him with it so there was no chance that he could see anything.

He was standing there, waiting for her touch when he felt just the tip of her tongue lick and lick the head of his now very hard cock. He was side-on to Caroline while Elizabeth was doing this, and she was watching every second of it and getting more and more turned on, knowing her best friend was about to take him all into her sweet, inviting mouth.

Elizabeth looked at her while she was exploring him and invited her over with a very quiet beckoned finger movement so as not to alert her pilot, who by this stage was getting more and more turned on.

Caroline joined her on the floor and not to give the game away, they never used their hands, just their mouths and tongues, taking turns to explore and take him into their mouths, but making sure that they never let him get too far ahead of them and cum. They kept speeding up and slowing down while running their mouths all the way down his shaft and being rough and gentle all at the same time.

He was starting to moan a lot louder now and was so enjoying the attention he was getting from his young companion that he didn't even notice that he was getting it from both of them.

Caroline felt him start to throb inside her mouth and she knew it was only going to be a few minutes away before he couldn't take anymore and lost control of his body and let it all go.

Not knowing how long ago he had had any, she moved away and let Elizabeth take over, sitting down again and watching her friend. Elizabeth went in for more but also realised right away he was about to explode, but she wasn't even close to being done with him yet. She slowed right down and got his body to calm back down a bit so she could have more of what she wanted. She was enjoying being in control and was more than happy to take the lead from Caroline's life and take advantage of her sexuality and be herself.

Caroline was enjoying letting Elizabeth have her time with her pilot friend and was living in the moment, knowing that she had opened up Elizabeth's mind to being who she wanted to be and not conforming to what society had told her she had to be and how to act.

Caroline was watching them both intensely and loving every moment of it, while making sure she was enjoying her own body at the same time. It was like watching porn but with the stars right in front of her; she could see the bumps on their skin and there was a smell of pure sex in her living room and it was driving her crazy and her hands were just making sure that she didn't go without as she brought herself off over and over again. She wasn't being quiet about it either and Elizabeth was keeping an eye on her the whole time.

Elizabeth laid her pilot down and took off his blindfold and positioned herself over the top of him facing away from him and looking straight at Caroline. Without hesitation, her hand slid between her legs and grabbed his throbbing cock which was still wet from hers and Caroline's mouths being on it and positioned herself right over the top of him and put his head right at the entrance to her now wet pussy while rubbing his head against her clit.

She wanted him so badly and couldn't stop herself enveloping him inside her warm wet lips and she let out a huge moan as she dropped down hard on him and engulfed him fully inside her. She let out a loud scream as she took him in and started to ride him hard while looking straight into Caroline's eyes and not losing contact with them at all. She wanted her to know how much fun she was having and for her to see that she too could be in control, that she had learned from her boss and was enjoying every stroke and every bit she was taking.

Caroline wasn't disappointed at all with her looking at her and was enjoying the sensation of being watched herself as she explored her own body while she watched. She was turned on so much and glad that she had consciously put Elizabeth on her list, even though Elizabeth didn't know it yet.

He may have thought he was the lucky one, but Elizabeth was the one who had decided how she was going to have him and how much he could have and if he could have her at all. This was the new and improved lady and she was going to take what she wanted and to hell with what people would think or say; he may have been old enough… *'Wait,'* she thought, *'how old is he?'* she stopped mid-motion for a second. *'Oh my gosh. What am I doing?'* She looked down at the older gentleman she was riding and slid all the way up, and at that moment, she exploded in orgasm and that was when she knew she couldn't stop, and she slid all the way down hard onto him again.

She was going to make sure he knew he had been had by her and every time she would slide upon him, she was making sure she slid down five times harder, making his body flinch and squirm under her.

Her hands were laid back on his chest to give her support and she took him harder to make sure he wasn't going anywhere or trying to move into him being in control. Also, she needed to stabilize herself as her legs were starting to shake even more now with the number of orgasms she was getting. He couldn't take much more and she could feel him starting to jerk hard inside her every time she dropped down onto him and she loved the feeling and it just made her orgasms even better and more intense.

She was young and stunning, and she was in her prime and wanted nothing more than to start living her life and enjoying everything that it had to offer.

As she dropped down hard onto him, she felt him thrust deeper into her as he exploded deep inside her body and she loved the feeling and rode him even harder to make sure that she got every last drop out of him. He grabbed her waist as he took her hard onto him and with one last huge thrust he shot his load into her and she screamed out loud as she orgasmed even harder and her body shook all over as it let go of any control she had left.

Elizabeth rolled over and laid down on her back next to him and just smiled and started to laugh to herself. She had not felt so alive and in charge for a long time and she loved the feeling. She turned to her conquest and looked at him, saying "The kiss was really nice, but the dessert was even better."

He acknowledged it and replied, "The best for a very, very long time."

With that, she asked, "May I ask you a personal question?"

He nodded. "How old are you?" It had been going through her mind ever since she slowed down mid-job and she wanted to know.

He laughed softly, "More than likely, I'm old enough to be your dad. I am 68."

Her face froze and she looked at Caroline. "Did you know how old he was before you invited him here?"

Caroline's mischievous grin was back; "Yes, I did. Why? Didn't you enjoy it?"

Elizabeth thought back to how her body felt and how much she had loved the orgasms he had given her. "I enjoyed it, but he is older than my dad, and I just rode him like he was in his 30s. If I had known, I would have taken more care and not gone so hard."

He smiled at her. "I wasn't complaining, and if you want to be gentler, jump on and try again. I won't say no." He laughed loudly with that.

She smirked. "Oh, don't worry, I haven't finished with you yet. You're sleeping with me tonight and there will not be a lot of sleeping going on." With that, she stood up and took his hand and walked over towards Caroline. "I hope we don't keep you up too much with the noise." They walked to the guest room and closed the door.

The following morning, Caroline made breakfast and knocking on the door, let them know and invited them to join her. About twenty minutes later they came out and they all sat down, had a great morning meal and talked about what they were going to do before their pilot had to catch his flight at noon.

He turned to Caroline. "Well, I think Elizabeth has worn me out a bit, but I still think I have enough energy for you if you want to finish me off."

Caroline laughed. "It is fine, there will be other times and visits, I am sure. If I am not mistaken, I think Elizabeth would like another go at you before you leave. Plus, I already had you in my mouth last night when you were standing up so I think you have been as lucky as you ever could have been already. Let's not push it too far. Plus, when I want you, I'll make sure you know about it."

They finished, cleaned up after themselves and went and got ready to leave so that they were not late for his flight. Elizabeth knew there wasn't a lot of time before they had to leave, but made sure she had him one last time when they went back to the guest room as she bent over the bed and lifted up her skirt so he could see she wanted him again.

It wasn't a long-lasting encounter that they had had in the living room, or the bedroom in actual fact, but she got what she wanted from him taking her hard from behind before they left. If nothing else, she had put a smile on the old guy's face and also, she liked having an older guy for a change and what he had been able to do to her that weekend made her think that, of all the young guys she had dated, none of them had come close to giving her the amount of pleasure her older pilot had given her. Maybe she had found the age range she needed to go for, or she could combine both a steady relationship with an older guy on the side, or just with older guys from then onwards.

She thought to herself, '*I have plenty of time to think about it.*'

They finished up and got dressed and headed out to meet Caroline to drive to the airport and say their goodbyes. Both ladies told him not to leave it too long before he visited again. Elizabeth had made sure he had her number before they left the penthouse, as she was more than sure she was going to have him again, no matter what.

The next day in the office, Elizabeth had a spring in her step and a huge smile on her face and Caroline was the only one in the office that knew the reason why. Her plan hadn't worked out the way she wanted, but it looked like it had made her look at her own life and take control of it.

Elizabeth entered Caroline's office and brought her a coffee and sat down with a nice sigh.

"Feeling alright, are we?" she asked Elizabeth, and it didn't take her long to just burst into a huge smile.

"Never felt better. He hasn't stopped texting since he left, and OMG I loved it! I have been going for younger men or ones my age my whole life, but what he did to me and made me feel was better than all of them put together in one. He is planning another visit soon, staying at mine; you should have joined us."

Caroline looked at her and just winked. "Maybe next time. We will have to wait and see; you never know, your luck might be in one day," and she laughed. She had already planned on something happening between them both just to try and see, nothing more.

Elizabeth went back to work and got on with her list of things to get done and contemplated the weekend and what Caroline had just said. Maybe she would step up and take control and plan something and not let Caroline be in charge. She was in charge of the office and work but maybe she needed to stop that and be on top for a change.

They had a busy few weeks ahead of them and Caroline had scheduled meetings as well that didn't include Elizabeth, which made her a little curious, but she didn't worry about them as she did this from time to time. Then, once she had things figured out, she would give them to her to fine-tune. She had been putting more and more onto her lately and making her run with some of the big business deals; she hadn't done this before, but she thought maybe she was just seeing if she could handle more and more of the high-end clients and getting her to learn more and be more in charge.

Elizabeth didn't mind at all, as she liked the challenge, and also, she admired the faith that Caroline was putting in her. She never once let her down, and on some occasions, had made more of an impact than Caroline had hoped for. She had closed a deal for a huge company that saved over 2000 jobs and within the first three months, had already turned a profit, all due to the structure that Elizabeth had put in place.

It was only brought to her attention at a meeting of the board when she was asked why her name had not been on it. Caroline thought the worst and thought putting that much faith in her had backfired on her until she saw the projections and the profit and turnaround; it had been miraculous.

She had structured it to save the jobs, profit-share among employees, kept the old board and re-educated them. She put them in touch with prospective clients and had been at all of the meetings between them herself. They had received over 200 new deals and contracts within the first two months of the restructuring and had to roll out a whole new production line. Caroline was commended with her choice of letting Elizabeth take more of a lead role even though she was her personal assistant.

Elizabeth did not dwell on it as a big success down to just her, the whole team had been involved and she had already thanked them all personally. Her phone rang and Caroline sounded a little off and weird on the phone and asked her to come back into her office.

Caroline got up and walked towards the door. As two of the senior directors left her office, they greeted her as they normally did and walked by. Elizabeth stopped and was a little worried. They never came down unless someone was in trouble or something big was happening, but mainly the latter and that had her worried. She walked in and the main owner was still in the office with Caroline and they were standing in the corner talking, with their backs towards the door.

Caroline turned to her. "Take a seat. We will be with you in a minute, Elizabeth."

Caroline had never been that frosty with her at all and that made her worry even more. A couple of minutes passed by and they returned to Caroline's desk and the main director sat down in the chair right next to Elizabeth, between her and the door.

Caroline picked up the remote and closed the blinds in her office. Elizabeth knew this wasn't good.

She sat down and started talking to the director in front of her, asking if he wanted to tell her or if he would leave it up to her.

The director looked at her and said, "I'll go first, then you can do the termination of her job."

Elizabeth looked shocked; she didn't know what she had done, and the director then started talking about the business that she had been involved in taking control of, saying that all of the meetings had been a success and she should be proud of what she had accomplished and the jobs she had saved. But, as per her contract at the firm, it firmly stated that only corporate titled staff members were allowed to sign deals and contracts with other companies and it had been brought to their attention that she was not on that list and had broken company rules, which was not something that they could overlook.

Even worse, he continued, was that as a personal assistant, even as good as she was, and the leader she was, it wasn't something that they could just brush under the carpet and he was sorry that there wasn't anything he could do about it.

He handed over to Caroline who handed her a letter signed by all of the directors terminating her personal assistants' position with immediate effect. Elizabeth sat there, shocked, and couldn't say a word. she had just been fired by the one person she trusted more than anything. She felt herself welling up. Just then, Caroline jumped in and looked at the director.

"Okay, enough. Rip that letter up, John." He reached across and took it from her and tore it into little pieces.

Elizabeth was even more confused.

"Okay… am I fired or not?"

Caroline couldn't stop herself from laughing and also welling up a little in the eyes.

John stood, "You need to come with us."

They left the room and went to the office next door to Caroline's and opened the door.

No one had used it before and it had been used for storage, but John opened the door and it had been cleaned out and was set up perfectly to match Elizabeth's tastes. She was confused now even more. Caroline peeled off the cover on the door to reveal

Elizabeth's name on it and new title. *Director of Acquisitions.* It took her back.

"I can't train you any more than I have done," she said to Elizabeth, "and if you are going to roll out more business like the last one you have done, then we can't have you as just a personal assistant any longer. So, we have made a position for you working directly with me. Your old tasks will now no longer exist, and you are going to have to find a replacement to do your job as well as a personal assistant for you. They will have both mine and your workloads to deal with and will have to work closely together."

Elizabeth walked into the office and just couldn't believe it. She looked at them in surprise.

"This is mine?" She burst into tears of joy and thanked them both.

They both looked at her and smiled. John cautioned her, "Don't thank us yet. It's a huge job and your first task is to fire two of the staff out there and promote them the way we have just done. It's not an easy job as you have to move not just the two you pick around, but also move all the others up and find two new replacements to fill the voids."

She didn't know what to say, she was lost for words.

"Can I just hug you both? It's not against company policy, is it?"

She wasn't going to care anyway; she had already been fired once that morning and they were getting the hugs anyway and she grabbed John and gave him a huge hug and then Caroline.

John blushed slightly. "Take the rest of the week to figure things out with your office. Your corporate card is in the top drawer. Get what you need, be ready Monday morning as you have a board meeting to attend." On that, he handed over an envelope to her and left the room.

Inside was a bonus check for her part in the company she had saved.

Caroline looked at her, happy and proud.

"You deserve it. But remember, it wasn't just you." As she said it, she looked out at the family working on all of the projects on the floor outside who were looking back at Elizabeth. "Never forget that," she said, while tapping the check in Elizabeth's hand.

She knew exactly what Caroline meant, and to be honest she didn't actually need reminding as she watched Caroline all of the time and had seen how she was with them and it was the way she would be.

"So, are you ready then? Let's go make the announcement to them." She walked out of Elizabeth's office.

They gathered the staff together and told them all the plans going forward. Elizabeth addressed the staff. "I will be sorting out the new posts soon. But in the meantime, I have another announcement. This bonus check I received will also be donated to all of you. Equal shares all around, but if any of you know that one of you is struggling or needs more help, then let me know after you have all decided as a group, not before."

She did this, as she knew some people were entry-level and needed a little more help, as it was expensive living in London. Most of them had been with Caroline for a few years and were getting very well paid and it didn't matter as much to them. So, she left it up to them as she knew what they would do anyway.

They went back to Elizabeth's new office and Caroline smiled at her.

"It's very nice. You should be very proud of yourself. But please, one thing to remember, don't get too comfortable, okay? There may be more moves in the future to come." On those words, she hugged Elizabeth again. "Oh and, find someone soon as I need a coffee." She winked and left the room.

Chapter 8.
The Weekend Away

Monday morning started as it normally did with Caroline getting in before all of her staff on her floor and made sure that she had stopped by and bought breakfast pastries for everyone and had the coffee ready for them. She may have been their boss, but every Monday was the same ritual for her, they did their work during the week that made for well-informed meetings so she was never caught off guard in them, so first thing Monday mornings, she would always make sure the office was all ready for them and for them to start the week off with a smile and in perfect tune with what needed to be done.

When all had arrived and everyone was in at 9 am, they would grab coffee and something to eat and head to Caroline's office for the weekly briefing on what was to come that week and have a quick talk around the group about what their weekends had been like and their families; she knew all their kids' names and husbands or wives by heart and that's the way she liked it.

She held dinners on the holidays for the staff
and their husbands or wives, not just to show that
she cared about them, but to make sure they knew they
were all important to her and each other. She loved
each and every one of them and if they needed
anything, they knew to go right to her, and she would
help in any way she could. The older people on her
floor knew they could trust her and whenever an
opening would come up working directly for her, they
would have so many people apply that she would be
interviewing for weeks before she filled the
position. Not that many positions would ever come
open, as no one really needed to leave or work for
anyone else. Her work weeks were always long and as
much as she worked long hours, Elizabeth was always
there to help out and wouldn't leave her office until
Caroline was leaving.

Elizabeth's office was right next door to
Caroline's and was just as nice as hers was. She may
have been her P.A. when she began, but now having
moved up herself, she had the luxury of having the

bigger office as well and her own P.A. Her new P.A. would still be treated the same as Elizabeth had been treated when she was in that position.

She was treated as if she was higher in the company, not only by the staff but by all the other directors as well, and this was because she knew what she was doing and was able to not just arrange Caroline's hectic work schedule, but on the odd occasion when needed, she was able to step into meetings and deliver knockout blows to companies when it was needed. She knew the ins and outs of all the deals and was an integral part of everything that happened at the firm.

This is what the two new P.A.'s would have to strive for and the level they needed to get to. Good thing for them, they already knew the ropes, as had been promoted from within. By the time Thursday had come around, Caroline had finished all the meetings that were booked in and was close to closing a few restructuring deals and had decided to take a short break for the long weekend and had picked Iceland. It would be a good break for her so she could see what else she could come up with on her adventure, so she rented a log cabin in the picturesque countryside about two hours from Reykjavík and decided to see what she could think of and what she could get up to while out there.

She arrived in the evening and it was dark and beautiful, with the sky so lit up with stars it was like daylight in her eyes. She hailed a taxi at the airport and a very young-looking driver pulled up and got out and opened the door for her.

She thought it was so nice of such a young man to do that, but then again, she was standing there in a gorgeous black and white dress and high heels, with her long platinum blonde hair pulled back into a tight ponytail and her stunning emerald green eyes hidden behind a pair of rectangular black-framed glasses that would make her look like every man's fantasy, no matter how young or old he is.

She slid inside, showing a lot of leg and she caught him looking at them and decided to make sure the ride to the cabin was as flirty as possible. She looked him up and down.

"I have friends who have sons older than you. But I hope you enjoyed the view." At this, he smiled, went red and closed the door.

She thought to herself, *'bucket list - very, very young taxi driver.'* She inquired about him as they set off and he had just got his license and was 18 and waiting to go to university in the fall. He hoped to get into a good company for an internship for the summers while he was there.

Caroline looked him up and down again in the mirror and added 18 into her journal; she knew it was a bit young, but she was doing this to open her mind and experience new things.

They were driving through the most beautiful scenery, with the stars lighting the way and she couldn't help but be affected by the mood in the stars. They continued chatting and like her usual self, she put in the smallest of innuendos from time to time.

"So, my young, fertile driver, how did you like the legs, then? Or are you too young and shy to tell an older sexy lady to her face?"

She could see him blushing and put her hand on his shoulder. "Don't worry, it's okay to be naive to think that I wouldn't notice you looking."

"I'm sorry, but I couldn't help it, they were right there in front of me and perfect."

She smiled. "Well, at least you're honest."

They pulled up to the cabin and he took a quick call. Caroline, thinking it was for another fare, let herself out of the door and went to the cabin. The door was unlocked already and the keys were on the inside table with a note saying 'enjoy your stay and we hope you have a good time trying the local culture.'

She smiled. "Oh, I will start with a young 18-year-old standing outside." He was still on the phone when she asked if he was bringing her bags in and he said he would and would stock up the logs for her fireplace, as was the custom to do for visitors.

'Too easy,' she thought. She went inside to warm up while he brought the bags in, making sure she was sitting on the sofa with her skirt pulled up as far as was necessary to show all her legs.

He went outside again to get the logs with a huge smile on his face and then she saw the light come up the long drive. She positioned herself so no one knew what was on her mind, the door closed, and she heard footsteps and voices. Must have been a friend of the driver's or someone asking directions, she thought.

She wandered around the cabin looking at the gorgeous wood that the cabin was made out of. Then she turned and saw the driver staring at her, waiting for her to turn.

"Have you finished the logs?" "No, sorry, that's my twin brother, he is getting them and will be right in."

Her jaw dropped, and heart raced; they were *twins.* The driver walked back in the door with his arms full of logs for her and put them down by the fireplace and lit a fire.

He closed and locked the door and turned to her.

"It's what you wanted, right?"

She smiled. "I was only expecting you, not your brother as well."

He walked up to her and placed his hands around her waist.

"Think of this as your tip." He slowly started to kiss her neck, then the other brother walked behind her and started to kiss the opposite side of her neck and she melted. She couldn't believe this was happening. She hadn't imagined it at all! Two guys were on her list, but not as young as they were and add to that, they were twins, this was well beyond her wildest imagination and she took it with open arms. She stopped them and dropped to her knees and looked up.

"This is on my terms and not yours." She started to unzip them both, freeing them from their jeans. She started to massage them both to their hard-splendid glory. *'Wow,'* she thought, *'they were so young.'* Over 30 years her junior and they were as hungry for her as anyone had been. She took each one in turn into her mouth and started to slide her tongue around their throbbing manhood. She was loving the attention and couldn't wait to have more.

She kept them waiting while taking her time to fill her deep in her mouth. She couldn't believe her luck; she had just crossed two on her list off and also added another one and completed it as well. What shocked her even more than having twins and their exuberant manner, they were devouring her body, was the fact that she hadn't planned on any of this to happen. Maybe this was the way to go with her list. *'Just let it happen.'* She caught herself as she moaned as one after the other, for what seemed to be two or more hours, they both took their turns holding her down while the other one went down on her, slowly parting her labia and licking her clit while the other kissed her and ran his hands over her throat.

She could feel his tongue sliding deep into her while his fingers rubbed her clit and made it throb even more and swell beyond her own belief. *'They may be young,'* she thought to herself, *'but they knew what they were doing.'* One orgasm after the other, each swap was more intense, each brother got harder and deeper into her with their tongues and fingers, each orgasm brought a louder and louder scream, her body was already exhausted, but they kept on going. They were like two guys that couldn't keep their hands off the most stunning lady they had ever set their eyes on and couldn't believe how lucky they were.

She was in a state of bliss; she had no answers for her body wanting more, she couldn't even fight back and get back her control as her body and her mind were already in places that she didn't think a younger man or men could take her, and she was now just a passenger for their needs and hers. She may have started this adventure deciding she would be the one in control, but now and again she liked being taken and having the control stripped from her, and this was one such occasion.

She didn't mind having her two young studs take turns on her, it just prolonged the erotic excitement of it all and was definitely one to be added and crossed off from her list. They had arrived at the cabin at 7 pm and it was already 1 am and she hadn't even had one of them yet. Her body was in full flow, she couldn't hold back the wave after wave of orgasms, They were not the best of lovers, being so young, but what they lacked in experience, they made up for in wanting her and wanting to please her; they did the last part really well.

It felt like hours they had been pleasuring her and it had been, so she decided that it was her turn. She stood up and pushed them both away and slid out of her dress revealing her stunning figure.

They both smiled as she walked back up to them. Turning her back on one, she bent over and took one in her mouth while she positioned herself in front of the other and told him to take her. He didn't need to think again about taking her up on her order and slid himself into her in one stroke. Her eyes widened and her mouth opened wide and he held her hips tightly and started to slowly take her. Each time he thrust into her, her mouth widened and she took more of his brother into her until she started to gag a little. The brother didn't stop taking her mouth to her pleasure.

She was in control, but they didn't know it, she was calling all the shots, doing what she wanted to do and getting them to do it without them even knowing. She had the art of this down now and was enjoying the control that she was having. The brothers were enjoying the time they were having with such a gorgeous lady. Even while she was being taken hard by them, she still had the air of sophistication around her and the beauty she had was just the icing on the cake.

The brother behind was holding on to her hips tightly as he neared completion and was now ramming into her hard and she could tell it wasn't going to be long before he relieved himself inside her. Her thoughts were that she was going to have him fill her up when her attention was taken in an instant to the brother in her mouth, and he grabbed her head hard and pushed himself all the way into her mouth as he came hard inside her.

She had no choice but to swallow his warm cum as he held her head in place as his body wriggled and he continued cumming hard, and with that, the other brother did the same inside her. She didn't know the feeling of having being filled up from both ends at the same time would feel so good to her, but she couldn't stop them now. Even though they were nearly finished, she was still having waves of orgasms driven by the young men inside her.

This was an unexpected start to her trip to Iceland and she wasn't going to complain about it at all, as she only had a limited amount of time to have fun and this was a great way to start her three days off.

After the guys had done what she had needed them to do, they all got dressed and she went to get a drink. They offered their thanks and made to leave, but not before both getting a kiss from Caroline before they closed the door and left. She stood there looking out of the window as the cars started heading off down the lane and went out of sight. She contemplated what had just happened and smiled and walked over to her bag and crossed off the younger guy and added twins and crossed that off as well. She looked at the list which was now growing and thought, 'I'm adding more and ticking things off before even adding them.'

She sat down and wondered if this was all to do with the sexual side of things or the liberating feeling that it was giving to her. She wondered if she could control her urges and use them to better effect to be the CEO and the sexual person all in one and still be liberated.

Caroline was having way too much fun doing this and she knew that she had already started Elizabeth down the same path, and she couldn't just walk away from it just yet without at least trying out her one fantasy with Elizabeth, now could she?

She looked at the bed and it was so inviting, so she just snuggled up and drifted off to sleep without a care in the world. Her body still felt like it was being taken and she was still having waves of mini orgasms running through her. Every time she looked back on what had just happened, they got a little stronger and she tried to put them out of her mind for a few minutes, but ended up thinking about them even more.

Caroline woke up the following morning. This mini-break wasn't about going out and exploring and visiting places at all, it was to do with her relaxing and just getting back to her centre and thinking about where she was going to be taking her career from here on in. She was amazing at her job and had made her bosses a lot of money and they had, yes, invested a lot in her and her projects, but those projects were still theirs. She had said to them once she had made it to the top, her next step was her own company and she was without a doubt capable of doing that.

She wondered if Elizabeth would trust her enough to give up everything she had worked for herself and leave if she decided to, or if she would have to go it alone and forge ahead with her venture herself. This was what had been holding her back; if she went it alone, it would be all on her with no one there to help, but with Elizabeth by her side, she knew she would have that encouragement to persevere and have faith in what she could do.

Caroline didn't have a lack of confidence. She was full of self-belief and knew that, once she set her mind on it, she would succeed, but she still needed Elizabeth beside her. This time, though, she didn't want to keep her as her P.A., she wanted to bring her in as a partner to reward her for all of the hard work and loyalty that she had shown to her for all the years that they had worked together.

She decided that she would sit her down and talk to her, but not before she had everything worked out. Her next week at work was going to be a very hectic one and she had so many meetings, so she thought that she would take the time this weekend to sit and work it out and figure out what clients to go for and how to structure the new company.

She knew that if she was to bring Elizabeth on with her, that she would have to have it all worked out the right way, as this is what Elizabeth did for her on a daily basis, so if she could bring it all together she knew the missing parts wouldn't take

Elizabeth long at all to figure out and advance the project to fruition.

That weekend flew by as she was making plans and storyboards, following how she saw the business going and the growth that she could foresee. She wasn't worried about financial backing, as she had worked with the banks for many years and knew that she had been putting in place a structure of valued clients and companies that would see the value in doing business with her instead of a larger firm. She knew she had the reputation to grow and restructure companies rather than breaking them up and selling them on at a loss and putting people out of work. She hated the companies that did this and always kept her ear to the ground, looking at the finances of companies close to the edge and who was sniffing around them.

This is why people loved her and were drawn to her and wanted to work with her. She was a people person and always brought the best out in people and also made sure everyone around her was well looked after.

She knew that with what she had in place, it was still going to be a long road to building up a company, but it only took one deal and the rest would follow. She had faith in herself and Elizabeth, but she needed to convince her this was the right thing to do.

On the flight home, she relaxed and just enjoyed the time she had left. Facing Elizabeth the following day was going to be weird, as she had all these plans but wanted to have that sit-down meeting only when the time was right.

It had to be done right; she wanted her lawyers there with contracts, she wanted everything in place that she could get done, she wanted Elizabeth to want to follow. She needed her there with her as soon as she notified her bosses and her staff on her floor, her family, the ones that had worked so hard to get them both where they were.

She would miss them all, but she needed to do this just as much as she needed her sexual and sensual side. She closed her eyes and just thought back to her taxi ride and her first night in Iceland and smiled and fell asleep thinking about it. She woke just before the plane landed and grabbed her laptop and made sure all of her research and appointments for her new venture were in a locked folder and password and pin-protected so that Elizabeth wouldn't see it till the time was right as she didn't want her to think she was leaving her.

She got through the airport and Elizabeth and her driver were waiting. They got in their car and started talking business right away. Elizabeth had booked in a couple more meetings with companies she may be interested in talking to and her week was now full. She thought to herself, *'Make sure if we start this new business, we leave time to be us and enjoy life, because there has to be a work-life balance.'*

She glanced over at Elizabeth.

"We need to start making sure we do not overdo our work life. We need to balance things out for us and ourselves. We can't work ourselves like this all the time as we will just grow up having only worked and nothing more. We need to live and enjoy life and what we have worked for, as it will be pointless working as much as we are and having no life to show for it."

Elizabeth nodded in agreement.

"Yes, I understand, but where did this come from? You have always been the bull in the business, going nonstop. What has changed? Or are you looking at just cutting back a bit and taking more time for you and your adventures?"

Caroline sighed, softly. "Changes are coming, and the changes will be good for all. It's time all my staff relaxed a little more and had more free time for themselves. So, the first thing will be that we are all having dinner out as a team at least once a week. Once anyone leaves the office, no one is to log on or do any work unless they have cleared it with me or you. That will only be granted if we are working with companies in different time zones."

Caroline was putting things in place right away in the hope that all her team would come and follow her, that they would know once she left, the next boss wouldn't be the same. She was aligning herself with all of her staff and that was the way she wanted it, as she had the best staff in her company, and they were all loyal to her.

So, if this venture was going to happen and when it did happen, she was going to make sure she had the best team behind her and the best chance of success.

Chapter 9.
Who was in Control

Caroline had had a gruelling week of meetings, between the stressful environment of the board room, her office and dealing with men in power trying to get one over on her daily. She was still thrilled with all the deals she had made that week. Her car dropped her off outside of her apartment building and she needed a drink. It was a Thursday, but she had no more meetings that week and she decided to relax a little and blow off some steam with her trusted friend, so while walking into her apartment building, she called Elizabeth and got no answer.

'*Strange,*' she thought, '*she never misses her calls.*' So, she tried again with the same conclusion to the call.

'I'll shower and call afterwards, and she may be free then.' She reached her floor and the elevator doors opened. She got out her keys and opened the door. Home at last, she sighed and turned on the lights and found Elizabeth standing in the middle of the room, waiting for her.

"I just called you. Why didn't you answer if you were already here?"

She never said a word but handed her an envelope. The room was covered in flowers of all kinds and it had a sensual fragrant aroma she had never smelt before. She opened the envelope and read it.

Caroline, this is a gift from me to you to say thank you for taking me with you since you have been at the firm and I also still owe you for my birthday surprise.

So, we have a car picking us up outside of your building at 9 pm and taking us to the airport where we have a plane waiting to take us to a surprise location; you will find that out on arrival. Go pack a bag and dresses and hot weather clothes and swimwear. Not much clothing will be needed. and this trip, I am in charge.

I have arranged all activities in advance, as well as some bucket list items to add as well as to check off. You have 1 hour to get ready. Caroline smiled at Elizabeth and walked over and gave her a huge hug and kiss on the cheek and went and packed.

This was a whole new side to Elizabeth, and she liked it, so, she went along with it as she needed a break from taking control of everything in her life; plus she didn't have to lift a finger as it was all planned out for her already.

Elizabeth was already dressed to impress in a long flowing dress that showed her figure and ample chest to the max, low-cut in the front, showing lots of cleavage to keep the mind wandering and the rest of the dress clung to her every curve. Caroline came out in her favourite dress that she had bought but had never worn. It was pearly pink in colour and with a low-cut back and crisscross design on the back. Side by side, they looked amazing.

Their car was waiting when they got to the doors and they made their way to the airport, and then to the private jet that was waiting for them.

All the blinds were down so as not to give away the destination that Elizabeth had arranged for them to go to. They landed about four hours later on a private airstrip on a Mediterranean island with stunning beaches, scenic hotels and beautiful villas that were dotted around the beaches. The lights from all of the exclusive resort lit up the night air with such a mesmerizing glow that you couldn't help but fall in love with the place. They stepped off the plane and Caroline took in the serene atmosphere and scenery.

A car picked them up and drove them to their villa, with its own pool, bar, waiter service, and maids.

Caroline's awe was present in her voice.

"How did you pull this off? The plane, the villa, all of it?"

Elizabeth grinned.

"I called in favours and this is just the start."

They went inside and were greeted by what could only be described as young Greek gods in aprons. They both looked at each other and smiled.

"Four days?" Caroline asked.

"Yep." Elizabeth stared at the Greek gods. "We need more time to devour all of the delights I have laid out for us. Like I said, Caroline, this is only the start. What you can't see yet you will see during our stay."

They decided a moonlight swim was in order and went and changed. They walked into the infinity pool, sank into the water, and relaxed as their waiter brought over drinks for them. They took the drinks with a wink and laughed.

'*Oh, this is going to be so much fun,*' Caroline thought and she surveyed what was on offer by the waiters as they leaned forward to hand them their drinks. The aprons were not hiding much at all. Elizabeth looked up.

"I don't mind if I do, thank you.," she said as she reached for her drink, but the waiter wasn't what was on her mind. She stood up and removed her bikini right in front of Caroline and gazed at her.

"Your turn."

Caroline obliged and stood up inches away from her and removed hers as well. Elizabeth didn't need an invite or anything else and she leaned forward and whispered into Caroline's ear,

"Add being intimate with your P.A. to your bucket list."

Caroline winked and leaned in, "It's already on there."

She went in for a kiss and took Elizabeth's breath away, Caroline ran her hands over Elizabeth's shoulders and down her now heaving chest as her heart raced. The kissing was passionate but deep, sensual and seductive.

This had been a long time in the making and had been one of the first things added to Caroline's list. It was hidden from Elizabeth but was there for when the time was right. With Elizabeth's back against the side of the pool and her body glowing in the lights, Caroline slowly slid her mouth down Elizabeth's chest and took her hard nipples into her mouth, playing with them gently at first, but knowing what she liked and how the touch of a person aroused her and her female body. She was better placed to send Elizabeth to places she had never been taken.

She was lowly flicking her tongue around and over her nipples, making sure to spend the same amount of time on each nipple and breast, caressing each breast with her hands as she went to work getting Elizabeth's nipples as hard as she could, knowing that she was sending other parts of her body closer and closer to being ready for her to explore and sending Elizabeth into waves of pure pleasure.

After slowly increasing her bite on her nipples, Caroline went in for the kill and put even

197

more pressure on her teeth to bite down on Elizabeth's nipples. In turn, Elizabeth let a pleasurable scream out of her mouth. Caroline kept eye contact with her continually so she could make sure it wasn't too painful, but just enough to make her moan in pleasure.

She slowly started to work her way down her body, taking her time to kiss every inch of her on the way down towards Elizabeth's now aching and throbbing pussy. She lifted her out of the water and Elizabeth laid back with her legs still in the water, Caroline parted her legs and started to run her hands from her feet all the ways slowly up to her thighs. Elizabeth couldn't contain her now increasing moans and Caroline's hands and tongue finally reached the now moist hard and beckoning clitoris.

Her finger slid inside her as she slowly went to work on massaging Elizabeth now throbbing clit. She moaned loudly as the first wave of orgasms hit and couldn't stop her back from lifting off the side of the pool as her body released her pent-up desire.

Elizabeth stretched out her arms above her head to try and steady herself and in doing so, her hands brushed one of the waiter's legs. She looked up and was in direct line of sight to his throbbing manhood as he had been watching it all unfold.

She craved to have him kneel down but couldn't say a word and just lay there enjoying each and every flick of Caroline's tongue on her and inside her, she let out another loud moan as she erupted again and again. She had lost count on how many and also the last time she had come so much and so hard; it wasn't as if she was attracted to women on a daily basis. She loved men, she loved the way they felt, their touch, the manliness of them when they would just take her and send her into heaven with their deep, hard, rough penetrating strokes that would make her feel like she was under his spell and his to do with as he pleased. This was different, this was sensual, erotic and seductive sex.

No deep, deep penetration, no hard thrusts, no rough manly sex, this was pure eroticism and soft lovemaking that she had never expected to feel like this, but she was loving every moment. While enjoying all that Caroline was doing, she couldn't take the waiting any longer and moved to stop Caroline.

"No, this is my time." Caroline looked up at the two waiters and playfully said, "Restrain her from moving." They nodded and knelt down and took hold of Elizabeth's hands and held them above her head so she couldn't move. This sent the next waves running through her body and she was now at the point where she couldn't control them. She was aching and her body was starting to lose all control it had over itself. The Greek gods, as she was now calling them, putting pressure on her so she couldn't move was sending her over the top.

Her ideas of holding and tying Caroline down was now the furthest thing from her mind. She had planned so many things she was going to do with her, and it had all been reversed onto her. Then she wondered, 'Was this her plan after all? Or was it Caroline's?' It was her list, to be frank, and she was the one that wanted to take control of her own sexuality. Caroline may not have planned this trip, but she was taking complete control of it now, and of her body.

Elizabeth had longed to be taken and to be held down, but always thought it was going to be a guy, or maybe two guys that would have done it. Now it was her boss, her confidant, her friend, and it was so erotic that she couldn't imagine it would have turned out this way when Caroline had first joined the company as head of development.

Now her CEO, her boss, was not just sending her to places she had never been before, but from this moment onwards, there was going to be a bond between them that couldn't be broken by anyone. She couldn't take it anymore, her back arched higher than ever before and she let out the loudest scream and she released the most body-shattering orgasm she had ever had. It was like a tidal wave of pleasure flowing through her body.

Each and every sense she had in her body now spiked to its limits. She was aware of everything, from each movement of Caroline's hands and her tongue to the smell of the ocean and the touch of the waiter holding her in place. It was so intense that she couldn't help but feel free from all the restraints that society and her job had put on her. This was her moment to express and release herself.

Caroline, at this point, had started to slow down on her movement and was concentrating on making sure she wasn't letting any of the orgasms that Elizabeth was having escape her taste as her tongue penetrated Elizabeth deeply. She wanted it all and was making sure that she took in every drop Elizabeth's body was releasing.

After what seemed like forever, Caroline finally gave in to her moans and released Elizabeth from her male restraints and let her get back into the pool. Her legs were like jelly and she was breathing so heavily she wanted a moment to catch her breath.

However, she decided to get her fill instead. She grabbed Caroline and put her against the wall.

. "Now it's my turn." Her voice was husky in Caroline's ear.

She leaned her back and skipped all the steps that Caroline had done and went straight for what she knew was going to be a soaking wet pussy. She parted her legs hard and dived straight in. Elizabeth's tongue slid deep inside her pussy and tasted the most tantalizing juices she had ever had.

She was rougher than Caroline, but that was because of what she had just been given by Caroline. She pursued her aim and got Caroline to have her first orgasm within minutes and that wasn't all. Once she had got her to her first climax, she got more intense and brought her to her second moments later.

Elizabeth kept up the pace until one orgasm rolled straight into the other. Her orgasms were ten minutes long and Caroline was breathing heavier than Elizabeth had been. She was squirming all over the place and trying to move away as each orgasm became so intense that they started to make her clit ache.

Elizabeth could sense this and was determined to give her the biggest one yet. She grabbed Caroline's hands and held her down. She pushed her fingers deep into her and she screamed at the top of her voice as finally, her body surrendered completely.

They both collapsed in a heap on the side of the pool and began gently caressing each other's bodies. They were only missing one thing - a hard cock to finish them both off. But their bodies couldn't have taken any more penetration than they'd already had.

They swam for a little while, chatting like nothing had happened. But while passing each other, they always went in for a kiss. After they had their fill of swimming, they both collapsed into bed and fell asleep with the thoughts of what had just taken place.

The next day they woke up early and had breakfast served to them in bed. They sat there, reminiscing about the night before.

"Did that really just happen?" Elizabeth ran a hand through her hair as she spoke. "You're my boss, I just made you scream so loud, and you went down on your P.A. How amazing was that!"

They both agreed, it could never happen again.

"Well, until the next time that is." Caroline flashed her mischievous grin.

Elizabeth had arranged a relaxing morning on the beach with cocktails. They had a glorious view of the ocean. They laid back, relaxed and let all the stress of both of their jobs just fade away. It was what they needed most. The two women had been working nonstop for weeks, and this was a welcome break.

This was going to be a calming weekend away from it all and nothing was going to get in the way of their fun. They went back to the villa for an afternoon swim in the pool. Each of them showered in the outdoor shower to get rid of the sand, stripped off and jumped in. It was pointless them hiding from each other now, with what had happened the night before, plus now they could get an all-over tan as well.

They both stayed in the pool relaxing and sunbathing. For their afternoon meal, they had a mouth-watering smoked fish dish. It was locally caught and cooked in front of them by their chef. Their waiters were on hand to cater for all their needs. The drinks were flowing freely, and they were enjoying each other's company. It was the perfect atmosphere surrounding them.

Both sat by the pool for a bit and then decided to head to the beach bar, which was just at the bottom of the villa's property. They ordered drinks and sat down at a table a few meters away from the bar. They chatted and were watching people to see if they could decide who was who and what their connection was.

While talking and having fun guessing what people were there for, Elizabeth spotted two young men at the bar.

"I would say first-time holiday away and they decided to go somewhere hot and expensive."

Caroline followed Elizabeth's gaze towards the bar.

"Hmm, best friends looking for an adventure and having fun." She winked as she stood. "I'll find out, stay here and watch."

Caroline walked over and went to the bar and pushed in between them to order a drink. She eyed each of the men.

"Hi boys, how's your first holiday away then?"

An expression of surprise formed on their faces. "How do you know it's our first one away?"

Caroline let out a soft laugh. "You've been standing at the bar looking at everyone, but without the confidence to go up and talk to them. You see,

I'm different; if I see someone I want to talk to I just walk up and do it. If I want more, I take it." With a wry smile, she turned and ordered herself a drink.

They towered above her, well over six feet tall. Both of the men were in their early 20s and both slim to athletic. With her standing between them they dwarfed her completely, but she now had their full attention. She got her drink, thanked the bartender and turned to walk back to her table with Elizabeth.

One of them stopped her before she went too far. "So how do you suggest that we approach a gorgeous lady that we both have taken an interest in?" Not knowing what the response would be they waited for her answer.

She put her drink back down on the bar and turned towards them both.

"Well, if it was me and I said I liked you both and couldn't decide which one to have, I would make a move like this…" Her eyes sparkled as she put one hand on each of their thighs and slid her hand all the way up grabbing them in her hand, gently massaging them hard until they were solid.

"Then, I would make my choice."

Both of the men were left speechless. She kept a hold of them, turned to Elizabeth and smiled. She turned back to them.

"I can't choose. Sorry, guys." With a gentle shrug, she let go, her fingers sliding over them one more time. Caroline took her drink and walked back to the table, winking at Elizabeth. As she got closer, she stopped, turned and looked at

them.

"I'll take both. You coming?" With that, she walked through the gates of the villa and the men were quick to follow. Once beside the pool, she let her eyes wander over their bodies.

"Well, what are you waiting for? The water is refreshing, jump in." She motioned to them and let her dress fall to the floor and dived in.

Both of the guys were in the middle of stripping when Elizabeth made her entrance behind them. Looking them up and down, she glanced over at Caroline, her mouth almost watering at the sight.

"Good choice; which one is first?"

Caroline put her arms on the edge of the pool.

"Oh, both of them, of course." She pushed off from the side, slowly swimming backwards.

With a nod, Elizabeth called to the waiter and ordered a round of drinks. The guys jumped in and didn't miss a stroke as they headed towards her. But she had other things in mind and stopped them halfway through their swim.

"Boys," her voice was commanding, her eyes sharp, "we will have hours of fun, I promise.

However, you are not in charge of this, I am." She had made them stop about three feet away from her.

As she moved back toward the side of the pool, she motioned for Elizabeth to join her. Caroline pulled herself up onto the side of the pool in the same spot that she and Elizabeth had had so much fun exploring each other the night before.

Elizabeth stripped off and joined her.

"Now, time for some fun." Caroline called over the guys. "We expect nothing less than perfection from you two. Until we are completely satisfied, neither of you will get what you desire."

The guys agreed and the women laid back and let them move in for a closer inspection of both of these sensual ladies. She and Elizabeth eased back and invited them in. It didn't take long before the guys were in between their legs and running their hands all the way up to them.

Elizabeth turned to Caroline, her expression relaxed.

"What a way to spend an afternoon and evening," she whispered.

Caroline leaned over, "They aren't getting any this afternoon. We are going to make them wait until tonight when they take us to dinner."

Elizabeth liked that idea and loved the thought of taking control of her own sexual nature. It had now started to make more sense to her why Caroline was doing this with her life and taking back the control of her own sexuality and not handing it the men in her life.

Too long had it been in the hands of men for all women, too long now had women been taunted with names and derogatory remarks. Double standards were a thing of the past now to Caroline and that's the way she was going to live her life. If she needed or wanted anything, she was going to take it.

The young men were enjoying themselves and both of the women were getting the pleasure they craved. From feeling the guys taking their time to bring the pair to climax with the touch of their tongues, and the hands running all over their bodies, they were still both in complete control of what they were going to let the guys have, and when they were going to have it, or even if they were to have it at all.

The guys were getting even more turned on as they switched partners and continued their talents on the different women.

'They're decent at what they're doing,' Caroline thought to herself as the other guy was now exploring Caroline's now very tender clit. He flicked it with his tongue as he sucked and licked as much of Caroline's juices up as he could.

These two young men were away on their first vacation together and thought that nothing could have gone any better on their first day in paradise than to be doing what they were doing with two very hot older ladies.

They were not exactly young, being in their mid-20s, but they still thought of them both as older women. Well, that's what they were going to tell all their friends when they got home. They would no doubt brag about scoring two enticing women on their first night there, and that they seduced them and had their way with them.

Nothing could have been further from the truth; the women were the ones in charge, and they knew it. They both thought Caroline and Elizabeth had had as many oral orgasms as they could handle before they would have to give in and have even more of them as their bodies would be craving more than just their mouths. The women stopped the guys.

"Would you like your turn now?" Caroline whispered.

They hoisted themselves out of the pool as quickly as they could and helped the women to stand. Caroline fought as hard as she could to not show that her legs were weak from the multiple orgasms they had been able to give her. But she was strong-willed enough to hide it from them.

She held each of the men's gaze, power and control cemented in her words.

"Gentlemen, we know what you are wanting right now, however, as we are ladies and the ones that call the shots, not you, we would like to go out to dinner first before we spend the night with you. That is our deal for you. You two take us out to dinner this evening and join us here afterwards and we can finish what we have started this afternoon."

They looked at each other and tried as hard as they could to persuade the women to let them try a little before that evening, but neither Caroline nor Elizabeth were budging from their choice.

The guys finally accepted and arranged to pick them up for dinner that evening and got dressed and left.

"I don't believe you just did that to those poor guys." A faint laugh escaped her lips. "Then they agreed to it, knowing we had already been pleasured and they didn't get anything from us."

"It's all about being in control, Elizabeth, and giving them what they really want, but on our terms. We get what we want first. They will be pleasuring us all over again, way before they finally get anything from us. If we let them have any, that is." The two women let out a long laugh and went back inside.

Caroline and Elizabeth made themselves ready in plenty of time for dinner, both taking the time to make sure that they looked immaculate so that the young men wouldn't be able to keep their eyes off them. They each wore dresses that barely reached mid-thigh level, and ice-pick heels. Caroline, as was her norm for going out, had her hair flowing down over her shoulders, while Elizabeth had her hair pulled back tightly into a high-fashion ponytail. They had selected to wear dresses with low-dipping necklines to show off their curving figures, and to ensure that the two guys only had eyes for them.

It was still Caroline's plan to make sure that they were the ones that called the shots, but she also had to give the guys something to look forward to as well, and to keep them wanting more. They left the villa and walked along the beach to meet the men, and they could tell by their faces that they were infatuated with the two heart-stopping ladies standing in front of them. They offered out their arms and escorted them to the restaurant that they had booked. Walking arm in arm, the guys were going to make sure they knew that they were more mature than their age. Arriving at their table, they walked behind the ladies and pulled out their chairs for them and made sure that they were comfortable before taking their own seats.

They had booked a table at a high-class beachside restaurant. The palm trees reached up through the canopy of the outdoor dining areas, and there was the ocean in the background. The rhythmic sound of the waves crashing gently on the beach set the tone, and its crisp white sand shimmered in the moonlight and set a romantic mood for the evening.

They ordered their drinks, chatted and got to know each other better. The entire time, Caroline knew that she and Elizabeth had them both where they wanted them. This wasn't a game to her anymore. This wasn't a case of, they get what they want, this was more down to her desires and if she didn't want it to go any further than dinner, then she would be sleeping alone.

She had to feel right about it and that it was something that was going to enhance her newly found sexual desire. For all the times that men had taken what they had wanted from her and left her with nothing but a sour taste in her mouth for her to deal and come to terms with, she swore she wasn't going to be like that. She always made sure they knew it wasn't a relationship, it was just a hook-up and she would never have left without making sure they knew that. She had been ghosted so many times, she wouldn't do that to anyone herself.

This was going to be one of those nights where Caroline had already decided once she sat down and talked to them that this was going to be just dinner, nothing more. She didn't need or want to sleep with just anyone, they had to have something about them, something that intrigued her to the point that she wanted to know more. As much as she was loving her newfound confidence and freedom, at the back of her mind, she still knew that to settle down with that one guy and have the sort of relationship you see other couples having was what she really wanted. But until the time when that one guy came into her life, she was going to enjoy her life on her terms and nothing less.

They had a great time at dinner and the guys were fantastic, but as per Caroline's nurturing nature, she made sure she took care of the bill and sat down to have drinks at the bar with the guys.

She wasn't going to lead them on or let them think they were getting more than they were. She told them outright that the two of them were wonderful and fun to be around, and they wouldn't have wanted to be taken to dinner by anyone other than those two. But it wasn't going to be leading anywhere and that she didn't want to lead them into believing any different.

The two guys, to her surprise, were a little relieved as they had been talking. They explained that they had had such an incredible afternoon with the two of them, they didn't want to ruin it by taking it too far. They so enjoyed the rest of their evening together, drinking and dancing that by the time they retired, and the guys left, it was the early hours of the morning and only a few left before they headed home.

The women took a walk together along the beach and just took in what an amazing time they had both had and what a magical place it was. They headed back to the villa to get squared away, packed and ready to leave. Just as soon as they were ready, the car was waiting.

They closed the door behind them and headed to the airport to an awaiting jet, both exhausted from no sleep the night before. They were both out for the count as soon as they took off as they headed back to London.

Chapter 10.
Her Phone Rings

Caroline was sitting in the office one morning talking to Elizabeth about projects needing her attention and sorting out which of her team should be assigned these projects, when Caroline's phone rang and she doesn't recognize the number. She handed it to Elizabeth to answer and she put it on speakerphone so they could both hear.

On the other end of the phone came a man's voice. Caroline vaguely knew it, but couldn't remember exactly where from. Then he mentioned Paris and Caroline started to realize he had found the note that she had left him. The ear to ear grin on her face said it all to Elizabeth and she told the man that if he could wait a moment, she would put the call through to Caroline.

Elizabeth put the call on hold.

Caroline lost her thoughts at the sound of his voice.

"What do I say to him?"

"Just be your normal self and be the new you as well. Don't give it all away from the get-go, and don't be too quick to jump in. What does this mystery man look like, anyway?"

"I'll show you." Caroline picked up the call while getting out her mobile phone and showing Elizabeth the picture of them both naked in bed together while he was asleep.

Elizabeth's jaw dropped.

"Good, lord, he is huge and built like a god."

Caroline smirked at Elizabeth's expression and focused on the voice on the other line. His voice was like honey to her ears. Her body began reacting with every word he spoke.

"I am curious as to why you left while I was asleep."

Caroline was finding it hard to concentrate. "I had to leave quite early that morning, as I didn't want a drawn-out goodbye."

He paused, taking in what she had said. "I supposed I can understand that. I do apologize that it has taken me so long to call you back. I honestly didn't know what to do. I was unsure if I was to call or just leave it to chance and hopefully bump into you in London." He cleared his throat and continued, "I'll confess, I tried to look for you in restaurants when I would dine out, and searched other places I thought that you may go to, but to no avail. I finally plucked up the courage to give you a call, hoping you would answer."

"Thank you for taking the time to call me. But I'm afraid I am at the office and I am extremely busy at the moment." She was trying her hardest to keep her thoughts in check. Her heart was still pounding from his call. "Is there something specific that you wanted?"

"I know you are working, however, the only number you left me was your office number." He was attempting to not let her casual dismissal affect him. "I was wondering if there was any chance that I could take you out to dinner or stop over one night this week."

"I will have to get back to you on the dinner invitation. As for coming over, that would be difficult as my P.A., Elizabeth, is staying with me for a while. I don't have the opportunity to be alone and talk. Also, you need to understand that Paris was a one-night thing. I still cannot believe I did all those things that night." Her voice was solid, but her heart continued to beat furiously in her chest.

He continued to mask his disappointment at her refusal, but he wasn't giving up. "Caroline," his voice went velvet smooth, "when I saw you from a distance that night, I watched you from the moment you had walked in, and I knew that I wasn't going to have left that night without at least trying to get together with you. My sole focus was on one woman. I only had eyes for *you* that night. I had been watching you carefully from the other side of the room the entire time you danced with all of the men before me. I wasn't leaving that ballroom without you."

Caroline was taken aback by his admission. She had been watching for him and she was shocked to find out that he had been following her. She was intrigued by that thought. Her stomach did a flutter. She quickly recovered from her surprise.

"I'll tell you what, Paris, I'll check my schedule and get back to you. In the meantime, I have quite a bit of work to do. Have a nice day." She hung the call up and left the conversation at that.

Taking the phone from Caroline, Elizabeth drew her attention.

"There is no way you are meeting him alone this time. I want to meet this guy in person and see for myself before you take the next step."

Caroline nodded her agreement. She knew she had to think about it first, to decide if she wanted to go down this route and meet her man from Paris again, or keep on enjoying her life the way that she had chosen to live it.

She couldn't help but think about every delicious inch of him and found herself daydreaming in her office on and off for the rest of the day. She knew it wasn't doing her any good thinking about him and what he did to her in Paris or what he could do to her in her office, or any place if the truth be told. Caroline thought to herself over the next few days about whether she was looking for a normal relationship, or whether she was looking for the same as she had at work, someone loyal to her and someone that would want her as much as she wanted him and to continue her new lifestyle together.

She wasn't sure about it at this stage but decided she didn't need to make a choice right away as she had bigger things to sort out this week and in the near future. She had a meeting set up over the next few weeks which would make her decision easier or harder on her new venture.

She sat back and thought to herself, *'This may all work in my favour. My new lifestyle and my new company.'* She contemplated combining them both and getting what she wanted without having to battle things out.

Her contract at her company was written the way she wanted it; it didn't stop her from leaving and starting up a new business in the same area, she had made sure of that at the time of signing. *'But how would I go about it? How would I get both lifestyles, and have them cross over? Also, how could I do all this with no one knowing?'*

The idea appealed to her but also made her intrigued about how it could be arranged, if it could be worked out at all. Maybe she needed to bring Elizabeth into the fold now, after all, they had an amazing time on the island together and she was sure she wouldn't just follow but also be her business partner. She still needed to get everything buttoned up and perfect before she let Elizabeth in on the business.

Friday morning came around and she was thinking about what she was going to be doing to relax and if she had any pressing plans at home that needed to be attended to. She picked up her phone and looked through her friends' section and wondered who she hadn't spoken to in a while. Most of her friends knew how busy she was and that she always reached out to them when she had free time.

She scrolled through and thought she had not heard from Emily, one of her closest friends. She didn't know when they had been friends, but it was long before she started at her firm and both were driven businesswomen.

Emily was a business owner in the medical field and was much like Caroline, always busy and working. She had built her business up from scratch and was successful in her venture.

Caroline gave her a call and waited for a little before she heard the calming and soothing voice of her friend; they chatted for a while and Caroline asked how she was doing and if she was still single.

Emily sighed.

"Yes, I'm still single. I'm taking my time to figure things out. I have loads of work, and personal time doesn't seem to fit into the picture at the moment." Her voice went a touch on the sad side.

This hit home as she was the same as Caroline, and it hurt her to hear this about her friend, even more so as it was the same for her as well.

Emily was elegant and gorgeous. She stood at 5 ft 6, slim but with curves in all the right places, with long brunette locks that flowed past her shoulders. She had the most alluring hazel eyes, and combined with her smile, could lock in the gaze of any man that looked at her, married or not, and they would just be hypnotized by them.

Emily loved her life and like Caroline, she had dedicated herself to her career. Caroline thought back to the phone call she had had in her office from her Paris guy. She still knew she wasn't sure if she wanted a relationship, but also that was way too much of a body to waste. A plan began to form in her mind.

The women both lived in London so it wouldn't be hard to set up a time for her and Emily to meet up, so she decided to do a little matchmaking, well more like a seduction on her part. The decision to meet up and have a drink over the weekend and catch up on things was made.

Caroline wore one of her favourite outfits. It was a long white suit dress, one piece, that had one button at the front, a plunging neckline to show ample cleavage, but still left a bit to the imagination. It was finished off with a high centre split and looked incredible on her. She finished off the look with a pair of Louboutin black high heels. She wore the outfit well; heads would turn and stare as she strolled by, and she would rival any lady that you saw.

Emily was just as stunning in a one-sleeve, off the shoulder dress that had a short, angle-cut hemline that flowed into a longer back of the dress. The cut showcased her nicely shaped and toned legs. She finished off her look with a pair of black open-toed Gina shoes. Both had their hair down, flowing freely, and they stunned everyone when they walked into the wine bar.

They sat down and ordered a drink. Caroline requested her usual wine and Emily opted for a pink gin.

Emily looked perfectly matched to Caroline in the looks department, and the only difference between them was Emily's eye and hair colour.

They had a great catch up and decided on a girls' night out the following weekend, as long as nothing came up. But Caroline already had other ideas after listening to Emily's dating exploits. Upon leaving. she sent out a message to her friend from Paris and asked if he was available to help her out with a friend of hers who was having a hard time in the dating arena and was, in her mind, needing a good date night.

She was adamant about making sure he knew it was not her, and he wouldn't be reliving his Paris exploits. She let him know right off that she wasn't in the right place for a relationship as she had a lot of things changing in her life and they all came first. He agreed to the blind date and to help her out and asked if there was anything he could do to make the evening go better.

They agreed on the following weekend and arranged to meet just before Emily would arrive. Caroline wasn't looking at this as a seduction date but was more inclined to think of it as a good match for her friend. Both had agreed that what happened in Paris wouldn't be discussed or talked about and that all focus should be on Emily.

Monday morning came and it was hectic as usual, and Caroline stuck to her normal morning routine that she loved doing for her staff, providing coffee, and this morning she had brought in a batch of fresh doughnuts for her team, as well as placing a little gift on each and every desk just to say thank you.

She had gone out and purchased everyone a dinner gift voucher for two at a top restaurant in London. Not only was it a thank you, but it was also a way to get them to have a romantic meal with their partners. Homelife to Caroline was a high priority. Even though she was single, she still believed in family life.

It wasn't just the routine that kept Caroline doing this, but she knew that if things went to plan, she was going to have the biggest merger of her professional career coming up and was hoping that her team would be following her. She was banking on this going ahead as soon as possible and still didn't know how she was going to tell them all, plus she had been away from her hidden life now for a few weeks and she was starting to get withdrawals from her alternative lifestyle.

She had started to enjoy the fact that she was high-powered in her professional life but wanted, and needed, more, and her escape from it all was her new life. She sat at her desk, took out her private laptop and started to think of ways that she could launch her business. A dinner party, a ball? She couldn't go down the masked ball route, could she? She could. She could get a five-star hotel and invite all her existing clients and her new ones and show them what the business could offer. Then, to top off the evening, have a blow-out ball, masquerade style, or even pick a theme for it.

Caroline wanted them to feel that her company would be able to offer more; she wanted them to know that she would put them first and make sure they had the best people looking after them. She decided that tomorrow was the day that she would talk to Elizabeth and tell her the plans that she had. But before all of that, she needed to relax and indulge.

She looked around for any invites and couldn't find one, so she decided to do a search of clubs around the greater London area away from where she worked. She still didn't find anything that she liked the look of.

Elizabeth came into the office and caught Caroline in deep thought.

"What's going on? You okay, need help with something?"

Caroline sighed and came out with it.

"I need to have some fun tonight to blow off some steam."

Elizabeth smiled, "I know just the place, be ready tonight at 8 and we will go out." Caroline smiled and thought to herself, what would she do without Elizabeth in her life and it made her more determined to have her on board. They got on with their work and ready for the meetings of the day. Caroline looked out of her office window onto the floor and saw her staff beaming with joy at the gifts they'd got, and the emails of thanks started to pop up on her screen. She loved making them happy and having them with her.

Meetings made the day fly by and everyone left when they were finished. Caroline went home to relax and change for her evening out. Elizabeth was waiting in the car outside of her building at 8, and Caroline walked out in one of her favourite black and white numbers, looking as gorgeous as ever.

This time they matched perfectly as Elizabeth herself was also in black and white. It was as if they knew each other too well, for they were always of the same mind. She loved the fact that their looks always complemented one another. They turned up at a secluded night spot in the country which was very well-presented, nicely lit up and exotic-looking.

They walked to the door and Elizabeth gave her name (which did not match her real name) and Caroline cocked her head to the side, wondering where she had taken her to. The doorman moved the rope out of the way and let them both in.

Once inside, it was a mix of elegance and burlesque. Caroline's smile grew and she loved the atmosphere that they had walked into. It was seductive with a hint of stimulating sexual desire buzzing through the place. The floor plan was spaced out comfortably, high-class seating all around, with nicely laid out tables adorned with a complimentary bottle of red and white wine.

The bar was tended by men and women and it looked like they served only the opposite sex when people went towards it. The place had been filling up and there were people from what looked like all walks of life coming through the doors. Caroline still didn't know what sort of place Elizabeth had taken her to.

"Where are we?" Caroline asked, breaking her gaze away from the scenery to look at her friend.

Elizabeth grinned and winked back at Caroline.

"It's a members-only club and just relax, it's not the sort of release you were expecting but it will be better than you think."

After a few minutes, the curtains opened and a lady walked onto the stage. The music began and the burlesque show started. Caroline couldn't take her eyes off the show. The singers and dancers were a joy to watch. The production took her back to the movies she had watched, and she had always wanted to visit a place like this.

The performers were all dressed erotically and had the most sensual figures she had ever seen. Their voices matched the songs perfectly; it was like Caroline had entered a new world. She couldn't stop glancing around and noted that everyone was feeling the same as her.

While her eyes continued to wander the room, she kept on looking at the young bartender who was ripped and toned and topless in his tight work trousers. She couldn't help but think about what she could do with him and what she could teach him. Her thoughts may get her into a little trouble as it was a public place and she had nowhere to hide her identity, but she thought, with a slight laugh, that it would be worth the risk.

She got up and walked towards the bar, the light hitting her black and white dress and showing her curved body. She didn't hide the look on her face towards the barman when she was approaching the counter. She made it clear to him that she wanted him and that she would give it to him freely. She knew that he must have these offers all the time looking like that and being in a place like this.

She sidled up to the edge and came out with it.

"I have a car outside, and I want to take you home with me right now and have my way with you."

He stared at her and didn't know what to say. He was shocked by her beauty and her forwardness.

"I apologize, miss, but this is my first night here. I don't think it's allowed under the strict rules of the club. I have to decline."

Caroline didn't hide her surprise, she just stared at him. She couldn't believe his answer. She asked for a pen, then she wrote down her number and her address.

"I am sure that after you finish your work you can drive, and I am sure they do not have any control over you once your shift is done." She winked and continued her flirting.

"I will say, they won't have control over you, but I will once you turn up at my address."

He took the note and placed it in his pocket, and she returned to the table to Elizabeth.

"Where did you wander off to?"

Caroline told her that she had picked up the bartender and pointed him out. Elizabeth's eyes went wide, and she just laughed.

"No, you did not!"

Caroline told her what she had said to the man and that she had given him her number and address.

Elizabeth was attempting to control her laughter.

"Do you remember I never gave my real name when we came in? You didn't ask me why."

Caroline nodded for her to continue her explanation.

"I did it because my younger brother started work here tonight, and you have just propositioned him! I came here tonight to support him on his first night, and you have just told him you wanted to take him!" Her laughter was unhinged now.

Caroline looked horrified. She was ashamed of herself and couldn't stop apologizing to her.

Elizabeth took a long sip of her drink to stifle her laughing.

"It's okay, I should have told you. I'm sorry, Caroline, but he better not turn up at yours tonight as I am staying in your spare room and I am not listening to you both go at it all night! But, I admit, it's great payback for the pilot you set me up with."

Caroline and Elizabeth laughed together and still couldn't believe that she had picked the one guy in a crowded place that was related to her best friend and P.A.

They got up after the last performance and went to the bar and paid their bill. Elizabeth introduced Caroline to her brother formally. Caroline couldn't say sorry enough to him and explained that she didn't know that they were related.

She glanced at Elizabeth, smiled and turned back to face him.

"You have my number and address; don't be a stranger and I still stick to what I said."

He looked at his sister and she shrugged her shoulders.

"If the woman says something and wants something, she always gets it."

Caroline pulled him over the bar and gave him a lip-searing kiss, bid him a good night and the women walked back to the car.

Caroline playfully licked her lips.

"At least he kisses as well as you do," she teased, as they got into the car that was waiting for them. Caroline felt much better after her night out, but knew that she was facing one of the most daunting days of her career by telling her friend and P.A. what was going to happen and that she hoped that she would come with her.

They arrived back at the apartment building and headed up. Caroline remembered that she had all of her research laid out on the table, and once they entered the penthouse, there was going to be no chance to hide it from Elizabeth. *'Perhaps,'* she thought, *'this may be the best time to talk about it.'* She still wasn't completely sure this was the right time, but she had no choice now and was worried that what she had planned for her venture wouldn't be enough to tempt Elizabeth to join her.

She wasn't her P.A. anymore; she had a position all of her own and was thriving in it. Caroline had warned her that day of her promotion, that she was not to get too comfortable as other changes were coming. But she wasn't sure that Elizabeth would be willing to give all that up now.

She had been in Caroline's shadow up until the promotion as such, and she was in a completely different role, but now that wouldn't be the case. She knew if she left the firm to take up this new venture that Elizabeth would be the one that would take her place. Could she really give up that chance to become the boss? To be her? Caroline knew it was a lot to ask of her.

They left the elevator and Caroline, somewhat nervous, turned to her.

"We need to talk before we go in. I am leaving the firm and venturing out into making a new business. I wasn't going to let you know just yet, as I wanted a complete proposal before I showed it to you. However, the research is all over the table and desk and I can't hide it from you any longer. So, all I am asking is that you take it in your stride and look at the bigger picture. This is why I have been having meetings that haven't been on the calendar for months." She unlocked her door and they went in.

The next few hours were spent pouring over charts and profit and loss sheets and lots of data, coupled with a few bottles of wine.

Elizabeth had already known something was up with Caroline a few months back, but hadn't realised this was what she had been planning. It was a massive venture, a little daunting to be honest, and the sun was now lighting the sky. She knew that Caroline would be wanting her thoughts on it.

She thought back to how she had been promoted and how scared she had been when they fired her, even though it was a joke. She raised an eyebrow; *'payback'* she thought.

She looked at Caroline, eyes wide, expression dark.

"Are you completely out of your mind?! This is a mess! Everything is mixed up, there is no structure, you haven't made plans for if it fails; I thought you were a better businesswoman than that and had your head screwed on the right way around!"

Caroline was stunned, as she didn't expect such a harsh rebuttal from Elizabeth. She thought that she might have said something along the lines of 'You have a lot more research and planning to get through, but all in all, it's a great idea…' Caroline's heart sank heavy into her chest.

Elizabeth glanced back at her and burst out laughing.

"Yep, it's not nice when it's on the other foot, is it? That's payback for the way you promoted me."

Caroline inhaled a deep breath and was so relieved Elizabeth was on board. She tried to calm herself and stop herself shaking. Elizabeth started talking and laying out what else was needed and said that the timeframe would be perfect if she did it at the turn of the year, as some of her projects she had been working on at home would be a great way to start.

"So," Elizabeth put her hands on her hips, "the question is, where do I sign? I take it you want me to be your P.A. again and build this together? I take it that is why you haven't shown me yet and had me help you get all this in order?"

Caroline shook her head gently.

"I didn't bring you in on this at the beginning as I didn't want you to choose between your new job and me. Besides, it would have been a conflict of interest and I didn't want you to be in a position of being liable for any of this. My contract states I can look around for ventures outside of the firm and go out on my own when I feel the time is right. Yours doesn't have that clause in it. Plus, your first-year contract is coming up in a month and you can leave if you want and don't have to think about any clauses. I don't want you as a P.A.; I couldn't and wouldn't expect you to drop back down. I was thinking more along the lines of a director, and business partner. I want you beside me and I want us to build it together."

Chapter 11.
A New Business

Caroline was meeting Elizabeth at a hotel for drinks after an important meeting with Caroline's new clients. They had just signed their first big deal and were celebrating its success. It was certainly a day to remember. Caroline had planned this for a long time and had her trusted friend on board with her, she had put everything she had into it and it was paying off right away on day one. All of her contacts that she had meticulously put together over all of the time that she had been with her old firm were working with her.

She had new offices, her staff had all come with her, apart from one and she was joining after the birth of her baby. Caroline had everything in place; they were not just employed by her, she knew their worth, they were family. She had made sure that she had given them all an incentive to join her, so they would all profit from the new business.

She was sitting at the bar waiting for Elizabeth when a man caught her eye at a table at the other end of the room. He was just the normal average guy, nice-looking and about 5ft 8, firm build. But there was something that attracted her to him, as he wasn't the typical guy that she would go for. But hey, what was normal to her anymore? She had pushed so far past her own comfort zones, that the lines were all blurring together.

She had barely made eye contact with him when Elizabeth arrived. They both had broad smiles on their faces. Elizabeth was elated.

"Well, it's official, I have filled out the paperwork, our first client is booked in and the bank have paid out, so we have our first venture and capital in the bank to push the business forward. We have officially arrived!"

They embraced and took a seat at the bar and ordered a bottle of champagne. The women tipped glasses to each other and had a drink to their new business future. Caroline picked up her phone and invited a good acquaintance of hers, Alicia, to come and join them as she had been doing a lot of the behind-the-scenes work for her on the new business.

Caroline had always made that call to her when things needed to be looked into or a more in-depth report done. This was the only person that she turned too; not only was she now a good friend of hers, but she was also one of the most stunningly beautiful women she knew.

Alicia was a complicated lady; she had been through many trials in her life. She was ex-military and kept those values still inside her. As for the men in her life, it was like Caroline's experience; they seemed to get what they wanted, then just vanish and ghost her. It wasn't that she had a problem keeping men around, it was just that she seemed to attract the wrong ones and would always be the one that ended up getting hurt. Alicia now kept them at arm's length and kept her feelings close to her. She put everything into her job and being a freelance investigator worked well with her features. If she needed any information, she could turn on the charm.

A lady with looks that were movie-bound, small of frame and a figure that was sculpted and perfect. She had a nice smile, flowing brunette hair and the looks that you only found in old movie stars like Audrey Hepburn or Ava Gardner. She had a classic, timeless look and she could get the information she needed without leaving the bar or meetings. Her body was stunning, not the way the other two looked, but it was perfect for her. Toned and slim, weighing about 118 pounds and with 34d breasts, she dropped jaws.

She arrived in a show-stopping purple dress and ice-pick heels to match. She took a seat beside them and with her joining, it wasn't a surprise that all the men in the bar were looking in their direction.

They talked for a few minutes and Caroline got her attention.

"We have had a meeting with the two partners and decided that for all of your dedication and the work you have put into helping us sort out our new business, we are giving you a bonus. We are sending you away to a country retreat for a weekend. Not only have you been so dedicated to our new venture, but also you have been helping me for years. We all agree that you deserve a break."

She handed Alicia an envelope with her cheques, along with the reservations, and gave her a hug to say thank you. Caroline was still glancing over at the man that she had been looking at when she had first arrived.

Elizabeth and Alicia both caught her staring at him and laughed to themselves. They knew what was going through her mind and knew at some point that she, or one of them, would be making an effort to get his attention.

They continued to chat at the bar before being shown their seats for dinner and making sure the waiters knew that this was a special occasion. Caroline made it clear that they didn't want any mediocre food, it all had to be the best of the menu's selection. Caroline knew that this wasn't just her work that had got them to this place, it was the whole team, that was why she had made sure there was a surprise for each and every one of her staff that evening.

She had ordered, in advance, from her favourite restaurant in London where she frequently dined. She knew the owners and even though they didn't do a takeout service, they were doing it this time for her. She had made sure that she knew all of her staff's favourite dishes and had them all delivered for the whole of their family to enjoy. This was her family and she would make sure they knew how special they were to her, since all of them had risked leaving the old firm and followed her. Nothing was going to be easy building the firm up, but she had a team with her that would make it work. They all trusted in her vision and every one of them would follow her lead.

It wasn't planned to have all women working at the firm, but that was just how it had turned out. She didn't have a problem with men and had her eye on a business intern that she had met on one of her trips away. She still had to wait for him to finish his courses and become available to work. The women dined and talked and enjoyed an enticing meal. They had loads to talk about, but none of it was to do with work. Caroline had got that out of the way before they sat down and this, they all knew, was a celebration, nothing more.

Alicia left earlier than Caroline and Elizabeth, as she still had some things to attend to the following day. She was also going to book her spa trip and said she would let Caroline know when she had the final dates set. She didn't know why Caroline needed to know so badly but said she would tell her.

She hugged them both and made her exit. Caroline still had the gentleman in her eyesight and wasn't going to let this go without having a little fun. She was going to bring her new business partner along for the ride, but this was a celebration time for them. It was their business and time to look forward to the future. For that reason, she decided not to go for the guy that she had been watching all evening, but she wasn't letting her average Joe, as she was calling him, go by the wayside.

She took out a piece of paper and wrote her number down on it and walked it over to him.

"I am sorry, I don't have time for you this evening, but give me a call next week and we can get together with my business partner. Have a wonderful night and I'll be seeing you soon?" Then she walked off and left the guy sitting wondering what had just happened.

They had planned a party for a few weeks down the line to launch their new business and had decided to have some fun with it and make it a costume party instead of a black-tie event. They wanted prospective clients to know that they were good at their jobs, but could also let their hair down and have fun as well. Caroline decided that was going to be her exciting night with her average Joe. They paid the bill and got into the waiting car and drove back to

Caroline's before dropping Elizabeth off at home afterwards.

Alicia phoned late afternoon the following day and gave her the information that she was looking for and also told her she had booked her weekend away in three weeks' time, which would be the weekend after the launch party. Caroline thanked her and said they would talk soon as she had other things that she needed research on. After hanging up, she picked the phone back up and called Mr Paris. He answered and she went straight to the point.

"Okay, you took me in Paris and pushed me to limits I had never been to. For that, I thank you, but I am a different woman now and I'm in control of every aspect of my life, so I have a proposition for you."

"Continue," Paris responded.

"I would like to retain your services. I know what you can do to pleasure a woman. I would like you to be at my call, 24 hours a day, if I need sexual help with something and I call you. You would need to be able to take care of it, and maybe, just maybe you'll get to have me again, when I say so."

He took a moment to consider her proposition. His honied voice replied, "What do you need?"

Caroline gave him the information and dates and who he needed to seduce and how long he was needed for.

"So, what do you think, Paris?"

"How far do you need me to go?" His voice was still soft.

"As far, if not further, than we did at the hotel. Yes, or no?"

Paris accepted and said he would do her bidding for her whenever it was needed.

"Excellent, I control you now. You don't do anything at all with anyone unless I give you the say so. Is that understood?"

"It is."

She thought she detected a hint of amusement in his tone.

"I will be emailing you the details. Send me an email and I will get you a corporate card." The call ended and she leaned back in her chair with a smile on her face.

Not only was she taking control of all of her sexual pleasures, but she was also now controlling the man who had controlled her in Paris. It would be just friends or her staff that would benefit from his prowess but also, she thought it could help tip business deals to go through as well. She enjoyed the idea of her controlling him.

It was getting late by this time and the new offices were empty, apart from the cleaner working away on tidying up the office. He was a much older gentleman who had been the caretaker for the building they had bought, and once the sale was complete, he was left without work. She decided to take him on to continue looking after the place. It was a three-storey building and the bottom two floors were filled, the staff and the planning department were on the second floor, and the third floor housed Caroline and Elizabeth's offices, along with the board and meeting rooms.

There were no doors closed at any time. She wanted it to be an open-door policy there so anyone could come in for a chat whenever they needed. She wasn't going to lose the family atmosphere that had got her to this place in her life; it had worked beyond measure for her.

She could hear the vacuum going and this was the first time she had been alone in the new offices since they moved in. After chatting with Mr Paris, she realised she was slightly turned on. She decided that she would play with herself and remove any pent-up tension. She had been good of late and hadn't tried anything new or anything off her list.

Caroline rose and looked out over the room to make sure the cleaner wasn't nearby. She walked back to her office and sat back in her chair facing the door to keep an eye out for anyone coming in. She opened up her legs and didn't take long to become aroused as her fingers started to explore herself. She was wet and getting more and more turned on as she thought back to the last time she played with herself. That was at the joint birthday party with Elizabeth, watching her while she was riding the pilot.

The memory of it made her even wetter but she didn't want to climax that fast. She wanted to be able to prolong it and when she did release, it would rock her body to its core. She closed her eyes and slowed down with her fingers and went back to remembering every touch and everything that happened that night. Her legs were wide open, and her skirt was hitched up around her waist. She had kicked one of her legs up onto her desk and was getting further into her sexual thoughts.

She was oblivious to the cleaner, who had entered her floor and walked up to her office. He didn't stand there and watch, he wasn't that type of man. He cleared his throat and knocked on the door frame, then turned his back on her so she knew he wasn't watching. He liked working for her. She was kind, always polite and not like a normal boss. She opened her eyes and saw him standing there with his back towards her and thought that is a true gentleman right there. Not everyone would do that.

She continued to play since he wasn't watching and asked him what he needed. He apologized and stated he didn't know she was still here and had just come in to leave a list of stuff that he needed her to order. He said sorry, again, that he had interrupted her and that he would see her tomorrow evening. He told her he would leave the list downstairs now, at reception.

"No, it's alright, give it to me now." She could tell he was shy, so she stopped playing and lowered her leg down before saying this, but she was hornier than ever having just been caught.

He walked in and she could tell he still had all his parts working as he was turned on as well.

'What a waste,' she thought, 'but I can't. As much as I need something to help me release, I just can't.'

He walked to her desk and placed the note on the top, right next to her. She was close to his bulging work trousers, and without thinking, her reflexes took over. She put her leg back up on the desktop, trapping him from going backwards. He didn't know what to do now.

She looked up at him and raised one of her perfectly sculpted eyebrows.

"I need help finishing, as you interrupted my flow. I think you should help and play with me."

She spread the leg that was on the floor so he could see exactly what she meant. He dropped to his knees and didn't need her to repeat the command. Not too many times was a guy of his age going to be asked to help his gorgeous boss in relieving sexual tension. He wasted no time in starting to go down on her. Caroline was finally having a little bit of fun after being good for the last few months while she got ready to launch the new business. She didn't mind that he was older, as long as she got what she needed right then. She leaned back and savoured the sensations he was creating.

He was experienced and she could tell that by that way he went to work on her clit and had her squirming in her chair. She had to reach down and grab his head and push it harder onto her as she felt the first wave of intense orgasm rip through her body. She didn't want him to stop. He continued the sensual flicks of his tongue to get her off a couple more times before he stood up and went back to his job.

She was slightly taken aback as she thought he would have needed taking care of himself, but he seemed like he was happy to just relieve his new boss and get back to his work. She sat back and gathered herself together. She picked up her bag and made her exit for the night, stopping to thank Mr Cleaner on the way out, then she got into the waiting car and headed home.

She knew the next few weeks to come were going to be intense, and that the relief that she had just received at the office was a welcome distraction. Plus, it was a luxurious feeling having that kind of experience going down on her.

'*Boy, did he know what he was doing. Hmm… more late nights in the office.*' She smirked at the thought of future encounters with Mr Cleaner.

The next morning, she arrived at the office early as they had people coming in to finish setting everything up. She wanted to be there to make sure that it was done to the highest possible standard.

Caroline wanted it to be an inviting office, but also hi-tech and contemporary. She wanted clean lines throughout the spaces and had already returned desks that had been delivered, because she didn't like the ones they sent out as replacements for out-of-stock items.

The reception was the first point of contact and that was her main focus today, because she and Elizabeth wanted it perfect. Caroline started sorting things out in the reception area when Elizabeth walked in and gave her the normal hug as they greeted each other.

Both women took a moment to gaze around and couldn't believe that this was all theirs. They understood now they had to work hard to keep it. Caroline knew that both Elizabeth's work ethic and hers was solid, and they would flourish and grow to be a company as big as the one they had just left. She parted ways with her old company with the respect of the board of directors. They had already signed a contract with them to do all of the work for them that she used to do. Outsourcing would be economical for her old firm, as they would have had to retrain a whole new section of staff. Keeping Caroline and

Elizabeth's company in the fold would save them money and still keep the best team on board with them.

After discussing how they wanted it to look, what fixtures they wanted to use, and the whole feel of it, Caroline headed to her office. She sat down and started to sort out things on her desk, as she still hadn't had the time to set it up like her old office. This time, it was even more expansive than her old one. Her desk had been delivered and she even had the space to have a comfortable, relaxing area. She had a couple of high-end leather couches delivered and it completed the look she was going for.

She started to clear her desk and noticed an envelope with a handwritten note from the cleaner on top saying, *delivered by hand last night, left it for you.* She looked at the handwriting on the envelope and it said:

A note from Paris,

She knew exactly who it was from and sat for a minute before opening it.

Caroline's letter

Dear Caroline,

Thank you for the call the other day and I am more than happy to do your bidding for you, when and if I am needed. I hope you realize what you are asking me to do is not something I am used to doing. I will do my best to make whatever you need me to do be what you expect it to be and more.

Saying that, I also want you to know what you are giving away. I have written this letter for you so that you will know what is in here will be exactly what the people you are sending me to seduce or meet will be receiving.

I thought I would sit down and write you a letter as I can't get Paris out of my head, the room, the elevator, the ball, it just brings back such emotions and pleasure that I couldn't help but put into words how much I long for it to happen again, so here you are.

I would start with your nipples and work my way up to your neck. Taking turns, sucking on each nipple and massaging your breasts. Then I would slowly remove your shorts and part your legs before taking a hold of your wrists and tying them to each corner of the bed.

Once I have done this, I am going to work my way down to your ankles and tie them to the corners as well, making sure they are tight enough so you can't move. Then I would take out the blindfold and put it over your eyes gently, making sure you knew what was to become of your body.

I would be exploring each and every inch of it so gently that with each touch your whole body would shudder in ecstasy. Once I had your eyes covered, I would brush past you with just the backside of my fingernails on different parts of your body, so you didn't know which area was going to be touched next, or with what.

I would use my finger, hands, tongue, a feather, a piece of leather. You wouldn't know which was coming next or where. Once I had you completely at my mercy, I would make sure that I brought you to such heights that with each flick of my tongue, or leather or hand or feather on your clit you would be tensing all over.

Just the tiniest of touches on your clit would send goosebumps all over you and send your mind into a frenzy, not knowing where I would be going next. My mouth would start to explore all the way up from your now soaking wet pussy and work my way up to your mouth where I would kiss you tenderly, sensually, so much that your lips would fall open and you would want to be kissed harder.

I would be making sure I had contact with your body, just so I could keep your senses in such a state of arousal that if I entered you at all, I could make your whole body shudder.

You could feel my fingers start to explore your wet lips as I start to slide them deep into you, making sure that I take my time and explore every part of your wet pussy. Slowly taking the time to lower myself down your aching body, I would stop and slide up to your mouth again, but this time kiss you with real passion and pleasure while I push my fingers deeper and harder into you. Now starting to slide them in and out of you with more of an effort, I take my time sucking and biting your nipples and sucking them hard into my mouth.

You hear me undo my belt and start to remove my jeans with my spare hand, then you feel my body against yours as I slowly take a position in between your legs.

You can feel how hard I have become as I start to push at your lips and slide my head inside of you. You can feel me draw back my body and you realize right then I am going to be taking you hard. Your breathing changes as you wait for the first thrust and my hips arch ready and as I slide forward, I stop and completely withdraw from you, just to prolong the tension between us. Your breathing slows down and you catch your breath. Your back flattens on the bed as you realize I was only teasing, until I take a second to prepare and with one deep hard thrust that you are not expecting, I push the whole way inside of you with the full weight of my body behind it, lifting your torso off the bed, but still being tied up, you can't move or resist.

You take the full force of me inside you and let out a slight but not loud moan, as you know this is the start of what could be something that lasts for a while. You try and pace your breathing, but I realize this and take you harder and harder with every thrust, making sure that I put every ounce of pressure into each stoke.

Holding your shoulders, I get the best leverage and force to pull me into you harder, and your breathing becomes more erratic. I can feel you tightening up your grip on my cock with your lips as you try and slow me down, but it is to no avail. I make sure that I am in control of you and that whatever I desire to do to you, I will. Your body is mine and I will pleasure it to the best of my ability but also, I will make sure that when I have finished,   your body won't be able to take one stroke more as you will be completely spent.

I feel your body starting to react to my forceful strokes in you and I keep going to make sure I get you so close to having a body-shattering orgasm, but not too close that I can't stop you having it.

I feel your body start to shudder and I slow down and continue slowing down until I have abated your orgasm. This isn't just about my pleasure, it's about yours. Your body will be craving to orgasm, but I won't let you just yet. I slide out of you and slide my tongue back down to your clit and massage it even more, making every inch of you so sensitive to the touch that when I reach up slowly and take your nipple in between my fingers, you can't help but to scream out in pure pleasure.

Your body is aching so badly to be taken and for you to give in to your desire of releasing an explosive orgasm that you beg to be taken again. I duly accept and take you with such force I think you will explode on the first stroke. Not wanting this to happen, I keep the strokes as deep as I can but with less force to make sure that your body is ready and at its most sensitive. I want you as aroused as possible. You can feel me throbbing inside you as I get closer and closer to the edge myself but I'm unwilling to cum until I have completely satisfied you.

I take notice of your body and what it needs and how it needs to be taken and adjust myself accordingly until I have it perfect. With each hard stroke, I bring you closer to your limits; you are now so wet I can feel that every time I slide into you, your body releases more and you are now at the stage that I would love to slow you down again but can't.

I can feel your every heartbeat through me as I start to ramp up the pressure one more time, now not holding back, each thrust is with all of my being and so deep that you moan louder with every stroke. Your body can't take any more as I build up and your body lets go with such a force, I can feel it flow all over me as I continue to fuck you harder. Not slowing my pace, your orgasm continues to grow more intense with every stroke.

Your clit is so sensitive that each time I bury myself back into you, your body lets go again until you can't take anymore. I unload deep inside of you and I hold it forcefully deep inside you as I cum.

Then I will leave you just as quickly as you left me in Paris.

Hope this will all work for you.

Signed,

Paris Guy

Caroline sat back and smiled as she knew that she had him hooked and that no matter what he said in the letter, he was aching to be back with her again.

Chapter 12.
The Vineyard

The firm was doing well, and they had been able to secure a few new clients, but also, some of her old clients had come to them for advice. They would then end up signing with the firm, investing heavily in them and growing even more. An opportunity had arisen in Europe and they wanted to put some feelers out before they took the step of investing time in the research to move forward.

Caroline's Paris friend was not just a normal guy. They had met in Paris while he was over there at his vineyard; he was already an established businessman, and didn't come from such a humble upbringing as people thought. He never threw it in people's faces and never put on the heirs and graces some in his position may have done. He liked the normal life, desired a normal-sized house, except for in his vineyard, where he had a charming villa in the south of France and it was set on a sprawling hillside close to the Italian border.

Caroline set up a conference call with Elizabeth and Paris and explained the deal and what was going on with the venture that may have come up. She needed more information on it before she and Elizabeth were comfortable with putting their vast resources into it. Caroline asked if there were any suggestions that he could think of to get some more details.

Paris eased back in his chair. "Everyone is more fluid with their thoughts and problems once they have a drink or two. So, how about I host a wine-tasting party at my home here in France and invite the people involved over? Then I would be able to get the information that is needed to either go forward with the deal or not."

Caroline always enjoyed a good party but neither of them wanted anyone to know that they were interested in the venture before they had done their due diligence.

"It's an excellent idea, but Elizabeth and I wouldn't be able to be there. I can have a member of my staff be at the tasting in our stead."

"Not a problem; send me over the details and I will organize it right away." He knew something like this would be time-sensitive. The bonus was that he didn't need to order in any supplies for the party since he already had everything he needed at the vineyard and on the neighbouring farms.

They ended the call. Caroline and Elizabeth walked downstairs talking about it and mulled over who they could send to the party. It wasn't a matter of trusting them to get the information, as they trusted every single one of their family.

"It is a business trip," Caroline thought out loud, "but it may be good for one of them to have the chance to get away for a bit." The women stood in silence for a few moments.

Then, as if an invisible light bulb had gone off on the top of their heads, they both said, "Robyn!"

Robyn had been Elizabeth's new assistant when she had been promoted at the old firm and had been with the company for a good length of time. She was small in stature and a delightful woman. She stood about 5ft 2, slim, weighing no more than 100lbs and with long blonde hair.

She was married and had 4 children and was, as far as people on the outside of her world knew, a happy person with a great home life. This was far from the truth, though, as things had happened in her married life that she couldn't let go of and she was trying her best to work through them.

Caroline and Elizabeth had sat down on several occasions and helped her deal with certain situations and given their support to her. She didn't make it known to a lot of people that she was in turmoil with her relationship, but when she needed help, she always went to her bosses, her friends, if or when the time called for it.

They called her into the boardroom and sat her down and asked her if she was willing to go on a business trip for a week and do some investigations into the new deal they were working on. They explained that they knew she could handle all aspects of the assignment and told her it would be a great way for her to start working her way up in the firm.

They told her they understood that she had a family to think about and that they would be stepping in to make sure things ran smoothly for her while she was away. Caroline urged her to think of it as a vacation away from some of the issues in her life as well, to take some time for her own well-being.

They all agreed that she could think on it for the day and to get back to them as soon as possible as things were already in motion and they need to move as quickly as possible. They would be needing to make travel arrangements by the end of the day.

Robyn was always dressed smartly for work but wasn't as glamorous as the other two when she went out. As she was leaving the room, Caroline stopped her.

"Robyn, don't forget, we are going to have to go shopping for a few new things for you before you leave, if you decide to go. New adventures require new clothes." Caroline winked at the petite woman.

This brought a smile to her face as she knew how the other two loved to go clothes shopping and that she would be getting a whole new makeover done by them. She left the room to call her husband. He was less than thrilled with the idea of her running off to France, as he would have to sort things out with the kids and look after the house by himself, even though she had told him that it would be taken care of. He just didn't like the idea of having to do more on his own.

She put the phone down and decided that she was going to do it anyway, no matter what he said. It was a career-boosting opportunity for her, and her bosses were putting all of their faith in her as well. She walked back into the boardroom to speak to Caroline.

"I accept the offer, and I promise that I will not let you two, or the firm, down."

Caroline was overjoyed at her announcement, picked up the phone and called her assistant and told her to book travel for Robyn. She added that they would be out of the office for the rest of the day and if needed, to call them on her cell.

Caroline swung by Elizabeth's office and pushed her head inside.

"Hey! Shopping!"

Elizabeth needed no further encouragement. With those words, she rose quickly, turned off her light, joined the other two and left the building.

They had lunch first and then hit the shops. It was a different way of shopping than she was used to, as her life revolved around her kids and making sure they had everything they needed, along with her husband, before herself. Caroline and Elizabeth knew it and made sure that she knew this was a business trip and that she didn't need to worry about the expenses as they would be covered by the firm. They assured her that she should indulge herself all she wanted. She wasn't used to this kind of lifestyle and kept picking up the same types of things that she had always done.

Elizabeth took notice and had to step in.

"Okay, enough." She took Robyn's arm and walked out of the store with them. She led the two women to her and Caroline's favourite dress store. Robyn's jaw dropped, staring at the delicate and fine clothing items lining the racks. They sat her down on one of the plush chairs and made her relax.

"We will pick the clothes, you can try them on and decide what you like, and what feels good on you. Do not look at the price tags," Caroline warned her playfully.

This is how it went for the rest of the day; Robyn walked out with so many bags and new outfits that she didn't know where she was going to hang them all. Not only did she have two dresses for the party just in case one got ruined or something spilled on it, but she had an entire new wardrobe of business clothes. She hadn't been shopping for new outfits in a long, long time. She kept her emotions in check, but she was overwhelmed by Caroline and Elizabeth's kindness.

They dropped Robyn off at her house and headed home for the evening, happy that they had been able to put a smile on her face. Robyn's expression of gratitude was not lost on them; they knew how important they made her feel. They hoped that they were changing her mindset to welcome in more fun to her life and enjoy what her career may have to offer. The two women knew she could go as far as possible and they had given her the proper encouragement to expand her horizons.

Robyn was due to fly out at the beginning of the following week. It had been explained to her what information was needed to be found out, but that she was not to let anyone know why she was asking certain questions. She needed to keep things as close to her chest as possible, as this could be a golden opportunity for the firm, and for Robyn. She was also told if this went further ahead, she would be leading the deal and that if they pulled it off, she would be overseeing all of the business involved from then onwards.

Caroline had organized a car to pick Robyn up at the airport and drive her to her destination. The driver wound the vehicle through the scenic countryside until they reached one of the most expansive estates she had ever seen. It was lined with vineyards that rolled along with the landscape, leading up to a handsome villa surrounded by an ancient brick wall. The scene flooding her vision was like it had been torn from the pages of a fancy photo book.

They pulled up to the front doors and were greeted by Paris and his staff. She was shown to the guest wing. Her guest room was bigger than her whole house.

She had a bite to eat at dinner that the chef had prepared for her, but it had been a long trip and she didn't have the energy to look around too much. She decided that unpacking and a bath would be all she needed to do that night. Afterwards, she completed her tasks, she laid back on the bed, took some soothing breaths, just relaxed and passed out.

The next morning came too soon and the sunlight streamed through the windows. It felt different being here than in London. The air was fresh and there wasn't the sound of any traffic and the smell of the fresh outdoors bounced off everything. She got dressed and headed out to find breakfast in the main house. To her delight, there a decadent spread laid out with different types of cheese, grapes and croissants, freshly baked and as warm as needed to be. The aroma of freshly brewed coffee took her to another level. She hadn't been this overwhelmed by her senses before, apart from her first child when he had released a runny mess of digested baby food; now *that* was overwhelming to the senses.

To Robyn, it was like being in a different world. Yes, she had travelled before, but that was when she was younger, and the name of the game then was getting drunk and not remembering much about it when you got home. She had since matured, and this wasn't like anything she had experienced before.

She finished breakfast and was deciding that she would take a walk around, when one of the farmhands came over and offered her a tour. She accepted politely in the broken French she knew, and he just smiled.

"No need to struggle with the words. I am English. The owner and his niece asked me to make sure you were shown around to get the lay of the land and see what we have to offer here." They were looking around and Robyn was in awe of how attractive the scenery was and how much of a different way of life it was from London.

They toured the wine-making facilities and made their way along to the vines themselves. They spread out for miles and were all in perfect rows. She could see the people out at the vines picking the grapes. It really was a whole new way life, but Robyn knew she was there for a reason and they headed back to the house so she could sit down and start doing research on the companies that she had been sent there to check on.

She got all set up and wondered how her kids were doing and how her husband was coping with it all. With an unladylike snort, she didn't care about how he was coping with it. It was about time he stepped up to the plate. But she was hoping her kids were doing alright as she had never been away from them for this long.

She knew if she got this all right, then she would be spending more time away from them and making headway in her career. She realised that, in a few years, the kids would be taking care of themselves and she would be then left trying to get ahead in her job. This was a perfect way to get the ball rolling. Robyn set out to do all the research she could for the next few days, looking for different angles that she could pursue to find the information her people back at the office could use to make this venture a reality.

Paris hadn't been there much, just fleeting visits and stopping to see if she was okay and if she needed anything. She looked him up and down every time he entered the room and tried to keep her expressions hidden, so no one knew. It was hard for her not to look and fantasize about what it would be like in this magical place. She walked the grounds when she needed to clear her head and always got straight back to her work. Three or four times a day, she would send reports back to the office with the information that she had found on the people running the business group and what they would really need to make the businesses turn around.

The next few days were the same routine; she got up and walked around and then spent the remainder of the day making calls, researching, and making files on all of the people involved. She knew that the in-person meetings would be able to tell her the most about people and how they could help them. This wasn't about buying the business outright, this was about investing and making it turn a profit as soon as possible by putting the best structures in place.

Friday night arrived and this was going to be the test for all her research. She knew who was coming and the ones that would be the best people to approach to get more information. She relaxed and had a lazy day; she had done all of her homework on all of them and it was now about getting the intricate pieces of the puzzle to fall into the right places to make this all work.

She took a lengthy walk in the afternoon, then headed back to the hustle around the house where everyone was milling around and getting the villa ready for the party.

Robyn had been to parties before, but nothing like this. She had been bought two dresses and they were completely different styles to the ones she was used to wearing. She was a normal mum and didn't go and lavish money on herself like Caroline had allowed her to. But this was, first and foremost, a work function, and she could enjoy it after she had gathered all the information that she needed. She didn't want to let the firm down and wanted to make sure she showed how committed she was to them and that she was able to do all that was expected of her.

The venue was in the main hall of the villa and was rustic in feel, but it had been transformed into a paradise of wine and cocktails for the evening. It was very lavish but also in keeping with the heritage of the property. Nothing was done that was over the top but it had an air of elegance to it, as well as a modern glow around it without it being gaudy. The tables were wrought iron with solid polished wooden tops that had been made from reclaimed wood from around the property.

Paris had made sure that nothing on his land was wasted and he loved the way his staff embraced the same ideas he had about repurposing materials. Even the tables' wrought iron was from old machinery from the days before he had taken over the estate.

The guests' invites said they were to arrive from 7 pm onwards and there would be a short tour of the production area of the wine, then a sit-down meal prepared from the produce of all the neighbouring farms and local stores.

Upon entering the vineyard, the guests would be taken aback by its charm and historic details. The winding track flowing through the vines that was lit up by solar lighting added a glow to the air, and made it look like a wonderland. The path wound its way up through the valley, with the villa and the buildings growing larger in size as the guests drew nearer to the event.

Trees, which seemed to reach the sky, lined the drive as you entered the gates to the main property and they had been lit up in pairs with different coloured lights. Once the sun began to set, those lights would glow brighter and enhance the atmosphere surrounding the property. Robyn had been walking on the main drive, as she had done many times on her visit. She smiled, delighting in the fresh air and the beauty that beckoned at every corner of the place, when her host, whom she had only ever seen for fleeting moments throughout the whole of her stay, pulled up at the front of the villa.

She had only seen him on a few occasions and didn't really get to converse with him in any way. She wasn't sure at all what relationship he had with the firm, but she knew he didn't work for it. Perhaps he was a friend of either Caroline or Elizabeth. Robyn got closer and that was when she realised she hadn't really taken any notice of him at all, as the only real time she spoke to him was on her arrival and one morning briefly when she was still half asleep.

Robyn was petite in size, so much so that the slightest height of average guys would dwarf her, let alone a man the size of Paris. He waited for her at the door and as she approached, she realised that she was eyeing him up and down and couldn't help but smile to herself.

He gave her a firm yet gentle hug in greeting.

"I apologize, Robyn, that I haven't been around much. I've been away taking care of some business dealings. I am sorry I haven't had the opportunity to sit down and go through things with you and give you a proper tour myself. I do hope that you have been made to feel welcome and have everything you require." She was taking in his velvet words, which washed over her like a warm bath. She was still admiring his stature; not only did he dwarf her, but she could have hidden behind him and never been seen again.

He drew her attention as he told her they would have a meeting shortly but that it would be easier if they made themselves ready for the party first and had a drink before everyone arrived.

"Please, come to meet me in my wing of the house for a drink after you have changed. I will have a bottle of my best wine ready for enjoying." She accepted his arm when he offered it, and they walked into the house together, chatting away.

Robyn wasn't the sort of woman that would spend hours getting ready for a party, but she did decide to take a little extra time getting ready for this particular event. This was her chance to shine and once everyone was gone, she could relax and have a little fun before she headed home.

She had a shower and then sat pondering what dress to wear out of the selection that had been provided for her. It wasn't her style to show off her body too much, as being in that situation made her think of her kids and husband first. She made do with her work clothes first and foremost and when the occasion arose, she would borrow from her friends if she went out.

Robyn didn't feel bad about it; she loved providing for them and it brought her joy taking care of her kids. But this was a special night as she didn't have to worry about snarky comments from her husband like; 'What are you wearing that for?' or 'You look like you have been dragged back from the brothel wearing that.' He wasn't the most supportive of husbands and they had been going through a difficult patch in their marriage as he was spending more time away from home and she was dealing with everything herself.

She couldn't remember the last time they had even been slightly intimate with each other. It had been so long that she could look back over the last couple of years, and not once in that time had there been any sort of intimacy in their marriage. She decided to put all that to one side. Tonight was about focusing on work, then relaxing and having a little fun.

She poured over the dresses one more time and picked the form-fitting white dress, that showed off her curvy body. It had a split in it long enough to show off her sculpted legs, and her ample cleavage was on show, but not too much to make her uncomfortable. The dress enhanced her curves well enough that people wouldn't have to guess too much what she was hiding under the fabric. She slipped on a pair of high heels to match her ensemble. She tousled her hair, fluffed and sprayed it in places so it would stay in the shape she wanted. With a few more pumps of hairspray, some mascara and lipstick, her look was finished.

She grabbed her purse and headed out of the door towards Paris' quarters to meet for the drink. She was a touch on the early side, as it didn't take as long as she had thought to get ready. But knowing he was a guy, she knew he wouldn't take as long as her, and she didn't want to keep him waiting too long. She knocked and waited, then she heard him call to her to come in and make herself at home. She opened the door and walked in and sat down, admiring the décor of his part of the house.

He walked in a few moments later and took her breath away. He was shirtless and well-groomed. She didn't know he had tattoos and certainly wasn't expecting him to be built the way he was. His chest was tight and the dragon tattoo on his abs highlighted how toned he was. His arms were detailed in tribal ink-work and he was the first man that she had seen in a state of undress like this apart from her husband.

She tried not to openly gawk, but could not help it. He poured them a glass of wine and walked it over to her and handed her the glass. They toasted and took a sip; all the time her eyes did not leave his body.

'*He would crush me if he was on top of me. Oh boy, how I would love it though. Mmmm the weight of his body on mine...*' She took another small sip of her wine as she attempted to keep her thoughts to herself and in check.

He picked up a white shirt and slipped it on and started to button it up, much to her dismay. He missed a button, she noticed, and reached out to him, purely from instinct like she did with her husband. She pointed it out and quickly readjusted it for him. He smiled and thanked her. She wasn't complaining at all as while she did it, she had made skin to skin contact with him and the sensation aroused senses inside her she had not felt for quite some time. Her body shivered, despite the rush of heat pulsing through her veins.

They sat down, chatted and she explained how she was going to go about getting the information she needed.

"I'd be lying if I said I wasn't nervous about carrying out the plan." She took another small sip of wine to steady her nerves. She didn't drink too much anymore, but the wine was the best she'd ever sampled.

Paris acknowledged her concern. "Want to know the truth?" His voice was husky, which made Robyn shiver in delight. "This is my first time doing anything for Caroline's firm, and I want it to go as smoothly as possible. I thought that it would be best if you were on my arm for the entirety of the evening. That way, if either of us needs the help, we're right there for each other."

Robyn wasn't going to complain at all about being on his arm and feeling his muscles under her fingertips for the duration of the event. The guests would be arriving soon. They finished their drinks and headed out to the main door to be ready to greet them. Robyn walked by his side and had her arm wrapped under his arm, holding him tightly, with her head full of thoughts about her task of acquiring the information she needed for Caroline. She knew it was going to be a good night and this was about to be a new start for her career.

The guests were greeted, and all arrived on time and the event was in full swing. Everyone loved the wine, the cheeses and the assortment of fine meats that were set up for them. A flood of requests and orders were being placed for the wine, much to the surprise of Paris. He wasn't expecting that to come from the event. He had only set this up to help Caroline and Elizabeth get the information that was needed. Robyn had done a fantastic job of collecting the details that Caroline required to further the deal.

Dusk started to shift into night. The lights shone brighter outside and transformed the landscape into a magical wonderland setting. Great care had been taken of all of the trees and pathways from the house leading into the vineyard. The driveways had been lit up as well, so for as far as the eye could see, lanes of lights shone the way as people milled around outside and took in the chance to walk through the vines in the fading light.

There was a romantic feel in the air. Robyn caught herself thinking and wishing for a brief moment, that her husband was there, then she harked back to reality. She knew, in truth, he would have already been in a bad mood because of what she was wearing and that it wasn't his sort of thing and he would have wanted to leave after ten minutes. He would never have agreed to take a stroll through the picturesque setting outside.

Paris caught her staring at the lights and the surrounding colours and offered to take Robyn on the tour that he hadn't given her. He insisted that she had gathered all the information that she needed to take back to her bosses, and that now was the time to enjoy the evening.

Picking up two sizeable wine glasses and filling them with the most aromatic of red wines in his selection, he offered one to her, then offered his arm.

"Shall we?" He gestured with his head to lead her outside. She didn't take an extra a second to answer him. She slid her arm around his as soon as it was offered, and they made their way up one of the paths in the vines that others were already walking through.

They chatted about everything and she still couldn't believe she was walking through such a setting with a handsome gentleman on her arm. To her, it was as if she was living a different life, one that she maybe had dreamt of as a young woman. She realised that she still longed for that life.

She knew she needed to change things at home, but this was a welcome distraction for her at the moment. She had watched Caroline and her lifestyle and envied her for it, but also realised it had taken years of hard work to get to where she was. Despite her children at home, whom she was missing like crazy, she still knew that she needed a life of her own when she returned. If her husband didn't agree with it, he knew what he could do.

She had lived too long now being controlled by him. He said things that hurt her on the deepest level of her heart. She decided that if he couldn't get behind her choices, he could leave and she would do it alone. Too much water had passed under the bridge now that couldn't be taken back. She wanted the best for her kids and if that made her work a little harder and devote extra time at work, she would, and he could step up or step off. It was that simple.

She snapped back to reality and saw she had not just been holding onto his arm, but all the time, she had been running her hand up and down it while the thoughts had been going through her head. They went through the whole vineyard and met everyone back at the house. The evening was a great success, and everyone had a glorious time. Many asked if he could host something more than once a year. Paris said it would be a pleasure and since it was his first event, and everyone seemed to enjoy themselves, that he would definitely do it on more than one occasion. He promised that all would be invited back.

The guests stayed around for another drink and slowly began to take their leave. The staff milled around cleaning up until Paris stopped them.

"We can do all this tomorrow. Thank you all for helping make this night a success. Now get some rest." Paris grabbed a new bottle of wine and led Robyn outside to the courtyard. They discussed how things had gone so smoothly that evening and that she had all of the information she had wanted to glean from the company executives.

Robyn was pleased with what she had accomplished; she had made sure that she hadn't missed anything and knew she hadn't let anyone slip by. She couldn't help but look at Paris and wonder what his connection to the firm was and how he came to be hosting this event for them. She also couldn't keep her eyes off his physique. She dared to dream about what it would feel like having him. Being married didn't stop her thinking about it and she wasn't blind or dead. She was a hot-blooded woman with needs.

They sat for a while longer and her host stood up and said he was turning in. He made sure she knew that she had the run of the place for the next couple of days before she flew out. He reiterated to her that she was to feel like she was at home and to enjoy the rest of her stay.

They both stood up and walked back inside. Her eyes feasted over him, and she still couldn't help but wonder what it would be like to take him, to be able to have control over that body of his.

She was starting to feel more alive than she had been in years and she loved the new sensations. She knew that things had to change, and she didn't want to keep going along the same old beaten path she had been walking for so long now. She needed more in her life now from her partner and would make sure she

took this experience home with her and implement the

adjustments she knew she had to make, even if it

meant moving on from him.

Chapter 13.
Woken Up

Robyn retired to her room with her thoughts and removed the dress and lay down on the bed. She was tired but still in a state of arousal, due to being that close to Paris all night. Her thoughts were running wild inside her head and she decided to let her emotions and lust take control of her as she closed her eyes and drifted off.

She was woken up about an hour later by a sound coming from the kitchen area and sat bolt upright as she hadn't thought anyone was there apart from her and Paris. She wondered if she had left the door open and one of the animals had entered the house. She got up and put on her short dressing gown and made her way to the kitchen. To her shock, there stood Paris with his back towards her, leaning into the fridge getting a drink, wearing nothing more than the day he was born. He hadn't noticed she was there, so she stood still and couldn't help but to look at his body and salivate at the thought of what she could do to him. Or, what he could do to her.

Nothing was hidden from view and she was still transfixed on his body as he turned around. She attempted to avert her eyes from his form as he saw her, but she couldn't help but continue to stare at him. He was taken a bit aback as he had thought she was in bed asleep and apologized for his state of undress. He noted that she wasn't worried or complaining at all.

He could see in her eyes the thoughts that were running through her mind, but for once, he wasn't sure of what to do as she was a married woman, so he was looking for her to make her exit. Robyn had other ideas as she stood looking at his perfectly honed body.

She hadn't expected him to look the way he did. The reality was ten times better than she had daydreamed, so she started imagining what she would love to have done with him and what she could do with him. Robyn was rooted to the spot and couldn't turn away and didn't want to. She knew she should pass this up, but kept thinking this was a turning point in her life. Did she have the courage inside her to take advantage of this opportunity in front of her?

It felt like they had been standing there for ages rather than seconds, when she decided to live. She took one step and during that step she let her dressing gown slip from her body and onto the floor.

This was her choice and no one else's; she knew what she was doing. She knew that she wanted it more than anything else. She wanted to step outside of the box she had been living in and her body urged her to explore what was in front of her. She had an insatiable hunger inside her that she hadn't felt for such a long time. She was taking that leap and nothing else was on her mind. She knew it was wrong, she knew the consequences of her actions, but she was living in the moment for the first time since she was a teenager and that's all that she could think about.

The only light in the room was that coming from the refrigerator and it was a warm glow, bouncing off Paris's body. She reached him in a couple of steps and didn't wait to have her hands on his body. She was aching for his body by the time her hand first touched him and her body quivered as she felt his skin fully against hers for the first time.

This hadn't been on the cards at all for tonight, but she wasn't going to let anything stand in the way now as she yearned for it so badly, she wanted him, and she wanted him now.

Her hands explored him like he was the first man she had ever touched. She traced his muscles so tenderly and was turning herself on with each second that passed. He knew what he was doing to her.

Robyn felt his nipples harden, and they were getting more aroused with every touch. He took his time letting her explore his body, letting her move down his body… she was now using her own body to explore and letting all other sensations escape. She was nothing now, just a vessel with all other thoughts put to the side, and she was just enjoying each and every stroke of her hand against his firm physique. She let her fingers do all the talking. There was a fleeting moment when her thoughts turned to home, but it was brief.

It was as if her body knew that her thoughts had briefly drifted back to her life at home, as it tingled with a sweet sensation that coursed through her and it seemed to encapsulate her entirely, along with the air around her. No more thoughts were to cross her mind except the carnal ones; this wasn't a time to reflect, but to indulge in *her* moment.

She marvelled at the tenderness and the incredible feelings flowing through her body. *'What have I been missing?' she thought.* Her breathing quickened as she lay siege to his body, pressing hard against his torso. She went in for a kiss and he didn't move away and accepted it with his full might as he took her into his arms and lifted her up in the air. This was the first time that she felt her body shake as his body pushed against hers. He walked her over toward the countertop and lowered her down and leaned her back as he started to kiss her neck, drifting lower down her skin. He reached her chest and started to gently explore her nipples as she lay on the surface.

Robyn reached out above her head and grabbed either side of the counter and gripped it tightly as she started to feel her body responding to his lips and exploration. He was taking every deep breath she took as acknowledgement that she liked what he was doing and then would go a little harder with each time she wriggled or moaned. Her nipples were so hard that with every gentle flick of his tongue and bite with his teeth, her moans were growing louder, and the tenderness was getting to the point that she couldn't take it anymore.

He could tell that she was getting close to not being able to take much more playing with her now rock-hard nipples and decided now was the time to make her clit just as hard. Her tiny body against his mammoth size was something that she had never experienced before, and she was loving everything he was doing to her.

She hadn't felt this way in forever and had never had a guy take as much time as he was. By now, it would have all been over if she had been at home and he would have rolled over and gone to sleep. But Paris, oh Paris hadn't even started properly yet and hadn't even reached her clit.

Robyn's body was heating up more than she thought it would, and then she felt his hands parting her lips and opening up her inviting labia to bring her clit, which was now starting to throb harder with every touch, right into the path of his tongue. The first flick was enough to send her body into spasms and her moaning turned to soft screams as he started to suck and circle it.

He kept a watch on her breathing for any sign that she wasn't enjoying it, but that was never going to be the case. He had honed his skills of going down on a woman while making love over the years, as he always wanted to make sure that whoever he was with enjoyed it as much as he was.

His tongue started to flick inside her as he began to ramp up his motion, flitting in between her clit and tasting her sublime juices. His hands wrapped around the outside of her legs and pulled her in hard to his mouth and she let out the loudest scream so far.

She was getting wetter by the minute and didn't know how much she was going to be able to take, but it was as if he was reading her mind. He slowly finished exploring her pussy and stood up and smiled and without another thought, he entered her with amazing force that made her scream at the top of her voice. It wasn't a painful scream, but one that she had been dying to release as she felt what she had seen and craved for from the moment she walked in on him in the kitchen. She had wondered what it would feel like and it didn't disappoint her in the slightest.

She was being spread wider than ever and the feel of his passion and his strength in taking her was more intense than she could ever have imagined.

She could feel every tiny motion and twitch of him inside her; it felt like it was in slow motion with every withdrawal and thrust back inside. She could nearly count all of the veins on the outside of him and felt his heartbeat through him. He was bigger than she imagined when she first saw him, and she wasn't complaining. More to the point, she didn't want it to end. His hands were now both on her breasts as he pinched her nipples to make her moan even further.

Robyn knew he could bring her to climax very soon but was holding back as much as she could. She was so tightly wrapped around his throbbing manhood that he didn't know how long he was going to last either, but he was determined not to release himself until she had. It was looking like it was going to be a battle of willpower, until he decided that enough was enough and leaned forward and lifted her right off the counter and pinned her against the fridge door. The cold on her back sent waves running through her body and he positioned her perfectly in front of him and lifted her in the air a little more, then released her so she slid the whole way down onto him and clung to him for dear life.

She knew what was to come next as he continued to do the same thing time and time again, entering her with her whole body weight, her legs wrapped around his waist and arms around his shoulders and neck and he started to fuck her even harder and deep than he had done on the counter.

Robyn had to release and she knew it; she couldn't hold back any longer as her body started to shake and shiver from the inside out as a wave of orgasms reached their breaking point and she let it all go with a scream that could have woken up everyone in the house if there had been anyone else there. Her body shook uncontrollably, and she became more and more in rhythm with him. She wasn't letting up and she started to ride him harder and use her body against him now as she wanted to feel what he had to offer inside her. She hadn't done anything like this before in her life, she had been the contented wife that did as her husband asked and took all of his shit; this was for *her*. She was going to make sure he knew that he had just had her.

She motioned to him to let her down and get on the floor, and he obliged. With the kitchen being open towards the sitting area, he moved onto the carpeted portion of the floor. It didn't take more than a second for her to straddle him; she put her hands between her legs and grabbed hold of him. She was tender to the touch. It had been a long time since she had anything inside her, and never anything with his girth.

She slid his head in and let out a slightly painful but pleasant sigh. She knew it was going to be sensitive and sore in the morning and right then as well, but she wasn't going to give up just yet. The light shining from the open door glistened on their bodies, both drenched in sweat. They joined each other at the hips and were one.

Robyn was riding with a deep, long motion and each time she sank all the way down, she moved her hips to take as much pressure onto her swollen clit as she could to maximise her pleasure. It was driving Paris wild and she could start to feel him throbbing and spasming inside her. She thought back and tried to picture the last time she had been in the throes of sex that lasted as long as this, and it had never been with someone built like this, ever.

Robyn was going to make sure that this lasted as long as she could and if she regretted it in the morning, then at least it would be something that was worth regretting. Paris grabbed her hips and started to move her faster and harder up and down on him. She knew he was getting close, but now she was getting to the point where she was going to release herself all over again and she knew that nothing was going to be able to hold that back as she finally felt him fill her deep inside. With that, she couldn't retain any semblance of composure as she let out the loudest of screams as she tightened around him and flooded his

cock with the most intense orgasm she had had that
night so far.

Her legs were giving in and shaking as the
power had been drained from them. Any woman, she
thought, can fake an orgasm, but the shaking and loss
of movement in her legs, no one could fake that. She
couldn't even balance on her knees as she dropped all
the way down onto him and collapsed on his chest. The
last motion of her dropping down made him cum again
and she felt him shoot deeper inside her again and he
held her all the way down onto him with such force
that she quivered deep inside.

The movement stopped and she just lay on top of
him for a while, both catching their breath, and
Robyn realizing that she was completely satisfied and
still as aroused as she had been before they had
started. Inside the seclusion of the farmhouse and
after all they had already done, her craving was
still there, she had time to make up for. Her eyes
locked with his.

"Now fuck me hard and take me again." Robyn wasn't holding back now about what she wanted, and she expected to get it. She told him this as she leaned and bent over. Robyn took hold of a nearby pillow in her fists and as she felt his breath behind her, hot air running down her back, feeling it on her sweat-covered body and on the top of his chest and on his stomach. She didn't want him to stop. Her face showed it because it was red with the passion that was all welling up inside her, red and filled with lust.

She grimaced at the cold wall which seemed to be closing in on her in a good way as his strokes became deeper and harder inside of her, just the way she wanted to be taken. Her hands stretched out and pushed up against the cold hardness of the immobile structure to help her push back onto him. All she could think about was the feeling of him filling her up and getting his hard cock as deep inside her as possible, filling up her body as much as she could take. There was nothing within herself now, just his throbbing hard cock and the nature of the way he was taking her.

She reached back towards him as if the only sense she had left was touch, and grabbed as much of him as she could to try and take him deeper. As she felt the thrusts get deeper and his body start to tense up, she turned his hips and felt her body full of electricity and so turned on and finally free of all of the shackles that she had been living with her whole life. She looked into his eyes and his mouth as he reached the sort of pleasure she knew she could give someone.

He looked so fraught, his upper lip pressed against his teeth, and she felt a pressure coming from his body when he came inside her. The jerk of his body and all of his extremities being rigid with the force of his orgasm, she ran her fingers through his hair and whispered, "It would be so much more rewarding if we got to do this more often," and he relaxed down onto her body. At that moment, she did not let the unadulterated lust, craving and the ecstasy of her uncontrollable passion overcome her.

She laid down with her now aroused body on his striving, toned frame, feeling so many emotions running through her, and the feeling of being more satisfied than she had felt in such a long time.

No, this wasn't love, this was pure passion; nothing more than two people enjoying the moment. This was two bodies bouncing off each other, and the divine feeling of them joining as one for a moment in time, insignificant to some, but in the writhing of the two it made sense to them, moist hot bodies entangled together.

This was divine lovemaking at its most sordid, and the most carnal pleasures that two people can enjoy. They embraced and leant into each other, and then she leant back, arching in the pleasure that had come before, her arms propping up her arched back. She let him continue his exploration of her body, but she was now breathing hard from the exertion that had been hours in the making.

His eyes were open while he was kissing her body and he saw her watching him. He measured his tenderness and touch as he started to build up his motion with his sweet kissing and his gentle touches. He looked at her as he explored her body, wanting to bring it to further ecstasy. She stopped him and pulled his head towards her and sucked gently on his lips and took time to explore his tongue and heard his breathing get more intense as she felt him slide back inside her. She felt the sort of breast slap that can only be felt as two bodies start to writhe in passion, when their upper bodies slam together and start to flow together in passion once again.

Her dreams of passion had been more than answered and pushed beyond any bounds of reality that could have ever existed in her mind. Her body was still quivering when she stood up and excused herself politely and said she needed to shower. She thanked him for an amazing time, then she bid him goodnight.

She left the kitchen and started to head back to her room, and then stopped. She didn't want him to think she had taken what she wanted and left, so she turned and walked back. He was still laying on the floor, and he turned to face her.

"I didn't expect that, and I wasn't looking for it. I don't want you to think I was, and I want to make sure you know how unforgettable it was. I have a life to get back to, but this moment is going to live with me for a very long time, so thank you."

"It was unforgettable, and I wasn't looking for it either, it just happened. I am thankful it did. It was an amazing experience and I am glad you walked in on me." His soft smile warmed her. Robyn turned and left and walked back to her room and closed the door. She sat on the bed with the broadest of smiles and her body still aching and glowing. She walked into the shower and rinsed herself off, then climbed into bed. She knew she had a long day to come and wanted to be up early and have everything sorted and packed before her return back to London.

She closed her eyes and re-lived every second of her adventure and was glad she had taken the chance to come out here and was sure that with the information she had gleaned from everyone would mean this was a start of a new chapter in her professional life, and maybe a little bit of excitement in her personal life as well. She knew that she had to come clean about her feelings and her stagnant life at home. That one night she would keep close to her heart; if anyone deserved an adventure and to jump outside of her box it was her, she thought.

She had given so much to her husband with nothing in return, but now she had something inside her that she could keep as hers and maybe, she thought, it would spur her on to change the direction of her life. She closed her eyes and fell asleep with the thoughts of her sexual desire and liaison running through her head. It made for fantastic dreams and she drifted off into a deep sleep.

Chapter 14.
Moving Forward

It was a rainy day in London when Robyn returned and got back down to business, writing up all of her notes and the list of people she thought would be the best to approach to get the proposed move to help restructure the company and to turn it all around.

Caroline was out in meetings with Elizabeth when she had returned and she was told that they wouldn't be back for the rest of the day. She had all the time she needed to get it sorted and as perfect as she could, still knowing that Caroline was going to make changes to it herself and run with it that way. Everything was going as planned with the renovations of the new offices and Caroline and Elizabeth were busy looking into more business acquisitions that they could hopefully put their unique branding on. Caroline took a phone call from her old firm and they were in a position that they thought she might like.

It was a massive firm, but it had the potential to be a good portfolio business for them that would generate good income. Her old boss had always said if she went on her own that he would help when the chance came up. Plus, he wanted to keep her on his side for when things came up that he needed her certain skillset for.

Caroline had set up the meeting and she and Elizabeth were en route to that meeting when she had another call from her old boss saying that another new company was looking into the same deal. It had been set up by the same person she had had a run-in with in front of board members at a meeting, as well as ending an interview with him. She knew exactly who it was.

Elizabeth was looking up his new venture and had a big smile on her face when she saw it was a new client base he was after. It wasn't like they were going to drive him and his business into the ground, but she knew that if they went to the meeting and they took what her company had to offer, it would be far better than what he would be able to offer them.

She had the backing of some of the biggest banks and investors in all of London. They had made a lot of money from her over the years, so when the chance came to invest in her directly, she had a line of investors waiting outside the door with cheque books open and unlimited funding.

Caroline knew her talents and she knew that no matter what, she would be able to just show them what they had been able to do in the past with companies, turning them around into profitable business in a short time. The challenge was getting them to see it from her point of view.

This to any business owner was the one thing that they had to do, jump in and trust her, as she had pitched so many times and had a great record for getting them on board and helping them. She had also lost a few and had to watch them walk away, then see a few months later that they had folded. She hated that feeling, knowing she may have been able to help, and they had refused.

This was one of those companies; they had come back to the table in their last-ditch attempt to try and save and grow their company. They had come in and knew that they would be taking more of a hit from the proposal than they had in the beginning. She was well aware of this, but she was in this to make money and grow her company, not to see others suffer. Getting her company off the ground was just one of the main things, but having other companies see her compassion and empathy towards them would be the thing that set her and Elizabeth's business apart from the rest.

The women sat down and listened to what they had to say and could hear it in the chief execs' voices that they wished they had made the deal the first time around.

Caroline leaned in towards Elizabeth and whispered,

"We could really help their situation and turn it around. But I need you to trust me right now. It will pay off big time in the near future."

Elizabeth's expression was of slight surprise.

"I *do* trust you with business, just tell me one thing. How are you so sure about this?"

Caroline looked at her and simply tapped the document in front of her, tapping directly on an intriguing name listed on the page.

"Him." Caroline grinned.

Elizabeth glanced at the page and matched Caroline's expression. She knew that name; it was one she had seen coming up on a potential deal. She knew what it meant.

"Okay, let's do this."

Caroline reached into her bag and pulled out the original proposal she had put on the table a few months ago, but this time she had headed it with her new company's name. She leant across the table, smiling, took a hold of the new proposal they had prepared, and picked it up to go over it.

This was what they were offering for assistance and what her company would get. She read it through and flicked her eyes up at them.

"What you're offering is twice as much percentage in the company and twice as much as we wanted in the first meeting and also triple on future dealings."

She continued to stare at them and knew they were on board right there and then if she signed it. They would make a substantial profit if she agreed to the deal and turned it around. She took a moment with Elizabeth, then leant forward to sign. Her hand paused, she looked at them once more, smiled and stopped her signature.

Caroline put her pen down on the table, took the paperwork and tore it up. Surprise flooded the expression of the group, as the blood drained from their faces. They realised that the chance had come and gone to work with her.

"We want more. Nowhere in this document does it say that you will adhere to the way people are treated. Also, the incentives that the employees would get in return are not listed." Caroline's voice was firm and cut through the room like a razor blade.

The CEO had a sheepish look as he explained.

"With the amount we are offering you, we just couldn't figure it into the budget." They knew they had lost her at this point and were considering keeping the meeting with her competition, the guy she had turned away from the interview months back.

Caroline put up her hand to halt their discussion, picked up the original document and handed it over.

"This, if you remember a few months ago, is the deal I put forward. We are all here to make money. However, before that can happen, we must turn it around. No business is bigger than the people that work for it. You take care of them and they will take care of you." Caroline was careful to make sure she made eye contact with each person sitting at the table before continuing.

"I will sign the original agreement if you stick to the deal, and I will install someone within to help with the transitions. You will put them on the board as discussed previously. Only ten percent of the business is owned by us, not the amount you have now offered, and giving away forty-eight percent of future business is not in your best interest. We will sign for ten percent, and no more."

They froze with shock and couldn't believe what they were hearing. She was turning down money to help save and build their company with a smaller return.

The CEO shook his head, squinted his eyes, and gave her a suspicious stare.

"What's the catch?"

Carline smiled and passed it over to Elizabeth.

"We want a meeting with this guy," she said, pointing to the name on the page, "nothing else, just a meeting. We get time with him, and you get your investment. We grow both your company and ours, nothing more."

Caroline took over once more, grabbed her pen and signed the document. She passed it to Elizabeth to sign and then placed it in the middle of the table.

"Do we have a deal, gentlemen?" They couldn't wait to stand up, sign and shake her hand. She had made a lot of friends in that short space of time. Those were the kind of friends she wanted. They would be the ones that passed her and Elizabeth's names around and told them how they did business. Word would spread that they wouldn't take advantage of people, and this, to Caroline, was good business. She had wanted to strike up a deal with them when she first spoke with them.

Now she had acquired more thanks to the meeting that she had set up, and that was worth more to her than the investment. They left the meeting and kept their elation under cover until they reached the car. Once hidden behind the tinted windows, they squealed with delight and hugged each other. This was a massive boost for them, and they knew the weight that this deal would pull.

Robyn and Caroline had time set up the following day to discuss her trip and what she had found out. Her previous meeting and acquisition of the company that they had brokered into the deal would be a catalyst for taking over assets in Europe and building her and Elizabeth's business venture further.

This was an enormous deal for everyone that worked for them, and they knew it. Every employee wanted to make sure all bases were covered, and they had everything set, so the meeting, and each detail that Robyn could provide, would be priceless.

Caroline and Elizabeth both knew this was the one they wanted. It was going to be the one, if they landed it, that would be the tipping point of staying at the lower levels or competing at the top of the ladder with the likes of her old firm. She had resources that she could enlist, and she was going to use every weapon (and she meant every weapon) at her disposal to make sure her family would be in for their first profitable year working for her. Caroline and Elizabeth made a few key calls and set things in motion.

This was not a man's world anymore, this was business. If she couldn't do the typical things like they did at midnight meetings in clubs and offices, with brandy and cigars, and hold talks to manage mergers, Caroline knew she would have to up her game and beat them to it before they hit the golf courses. She would have to bring to the forefront her past work ethics and experience with the companies that she had turned around and make them focus on that.

Caroline needed a little pick-me-up. There was nothing that was going to satisfy her more than spending time with the one person that could take her to another level of sexual pleasure. She picked up her phone and sent him a message, hoping he would be free so they could have dinner together. In truth, it was the dessert that was on Caroline's mind.

She slicked her tongue along her bottom lip while delving into the memory of what he had done to her in Paris. She was longing to have him again but didn't want to give out the wrong impression that she was looking for more. She was enjoying her life as it was, nothing further.

Their business was taking off and she was having more fun than she could remember having in a long time. She had Elizabeth involved in her life and their friendship was bonded more solidly than ever. Nothing was going to change her mind on that. She didn't have to wait long until she had a reply. He would be in town in two days' time, so if she could

356

wait for dinner until then, he would be pleased to join her.

She responded and said she would book a table, send the details and meet him there. Caroline smiled to herself; she knew he would be wanting more of the same and she was in a place where she needed it as well. She was in control of her entire life, except her sex life; that it seemed, was still out of her hands. She couldn't help the cravings she was having. She burned to experience more of the erotic pleasures

which that portion of life had to offer.

Caroline booked a restaurant and a hotel suite. She was keeping her home to herself and only for special occasions. He was just a friend with benefits at the moment, and she wanted to keep it that way.

She didn't see herself settling down with him, or anyone in the coming future, but she still didn't rule out one day having that special someone to come home to.

She headed back to the office as she had to have a sit-down with Robyn and Elizabeth about the proposal for the business she had been sent out to gain. Elizabeth took a call and it was from the group they had just met.

The board had set up a meeting for the following week with the man that Caroline had wanted to meet. With Robyn's information and the upcoming meeting, they could be one giant step closer to securing the deal ahead of anyone.

No need to beat the other companies at their own game, it was just about being in business with the right people at the right time. The women were all smiles when they arrived at the office. This would be the first time they had set eyes on it after all the renovations were completed. They didn't want to have a sterile environment, they wanted it to be welcoming, yet with a professional atmosphere. The desks were laid out in an open-plan manner, as all the employees got along with one another. Caroline and Elizabeth knew that even ten minutes away from their desks, conversing with each other, brought them closer together as a team, and as a family.

Never did she have to ask people to stay on top of a project. Yes, they had a friendly environment, chats and lunches delivered, and would all take longer breaks than most offices would typically allow, however, they seemed to get even more work accomplished than anyone Caroline and Elizabeth had seen in an office setting.

Not only did they stay on target with deadlines, but everything that was required for a deal was always there a day in advance, before they actually needed it. Her team naturally ran ahead of schedule in case something was bumped up to an earlier date, always ensuring Caroline was never without the necessary material to close a deal.

As they entered the main doors, it felt like their first day at a new job; everything was completed and running. A flood of accomplishment coursed through their bodies as they took in the new look of the interior. With a spring in her step, Caroline went to the fridge in her office and grabbed four bottles of champagne to toast with her staff. She brought them down and Elizabeth called everyone over, giving a little speech before handing the floor over to Caroline. She took a moment to glance at her staff. The pride she felt was beyond any words she knew. Her dreams were becoming reality. She softly cleared her throat and knew that her words were about to send a shockwave throughout her people.

"As you all know, Elizabeth and myself have decided that since we get the companies we work with to bring their employees into the fold and give them a share or a bonus, we have decided that we are going to do more." She paused for effect. The room was silent as everyone waited in anticipation. The electricity in the air was tangible.

"We decided that everyone will get shares in the company, as well as whatever job you are working on for us, if we take over or invest in that business. You will then take a share in that as well and be more involved going forward in it."

An eruption of cheers exploded from her staff. Glasses clinked and a buzz of chatter rang through the air. After their drinks, Caroline sent everyone off for the evening and requested that Robyn come in a little earlier the next day to discuss her Paris trip.

They both sat in their offices and started going through the paperwork that Robyn had collected and researched while she was on her travels. They wanted to make sure that if they had any questions on the details, that they had them ready for the meeting. Robyn's work was detailed as usual, and they were not going to have too many questions for her. She was thorough and didn't leave any stone unturned.

They had an enormous amount of praise at the end of it for Paris. He had played a pivotal role in introducing her to all the contacts that she needed to meet. It was a glowing account on how much he had helped, and she was looking forward to working closely in the future with him again, if the occasion arose.

Elizabeth paused while reading the kind words about Paris.

"Did she… do you think she…?"

Caroline's wicked grin spread across her lips.

"If she did, I am sure she knew what she was doing. I am almost positive that she had a fabulous time." She sighed, looking back on her own memories. The aching desire to have someone inside of her again coursed through her body. "We are all human and you know her situation. Maybe it will be a platform to let her take control of her own life. Perhaps it will get her back to being the bright spark that we decided to employ all those years ago when we first started."

Elizabeth raised her eyebrows. "Sounds like I am the only one missing out with him. It seems that

everyone else is having a romantic rendezvous with
him and I haven't as yet. I'll confess, I'm jealous."

Caroline chuckled. "You are aware that your own
rendezvous can be arranged, right?"

Sharing a laugh, they cleared the cups and
party remnants and headed home, continuing to poke
fun at Elizabeth's jealousy on the way out. Caroline
pushed the fact that he would be in town soon.

"Stop your crying." She laughed, "I have his
ear and can sort something out."

Chapter 15.
The Meeting of Minds and Body

Caroline had been working hard all week and it was coming to a close for her with only one meeting left with Robyn and Elizabeth. After that, she could relax and have her long-awaited meal with Paris. The women arrived early and got straight into the details, but not before the coffee had time to take effect. They had each been focused on their work with long days and burning the midnight oil, but they knew the hard work was worth the payoff in the end.

They went through all the paperwork and charts that Robyn had put together, and as per her usual style, it was thoroughly researched and presented well. Neither Caroline nor Elizabeth disturbed her while she was talking about the main layers to the business and all of the people that they would need to get on their side. The major concern Robyn pointed out was that they needed to understand that the business was haemorrhaging money and needed a complete restructure.

Robyn had already drawn up the plan and executed it in a file to show what could happen to the business if they turned it around through their know-how and expertise.

Caroline shifted her eyes over to Elizabeth, a proud smile forming on their faces.

Elizabeth focused her attention on Robyn again.

"We already looked over the details last night. Robyn, you have done excellent work. Caroline and I have decided this should be yours to run with. All the meetings will be in your hands and we will be there just to get the deal done." Elizabeth was impressed with Robyn beyond measure as she continued. "If, excuse me, *when*, we get the deal done, we will be installing you as director and you'll have to take on that portion of the job as well as the other tasks you do here. So, like it was done to me when I got my promotion, you will need to find a replacement for yourself. Anyone inside can be considered, or anyone on the outside that you think could enhance and give something to the company is welcome. Just keep in mind that we have always promoted from within first. Remember this is all hanging on the fact that we get the deal done. I have every confidence that it will be completed, but keep working hard on it and use any resources you need to get more information to solidify the agreement."

Robyn could hardly contain her enthusiasm. She was about to jump up and leave when Caroline stopped her, closed the files and folders and focused her gaze on the young woman.

"Hold on, Robyn," Caroline spoke softly. "Now that business is out of the way, let's talk about France, shall we?"

Robyn knew exactly what she was talking about and was hoping that she hadn't overstepped her role with doing what she did that night. It was apparent that Paris was a friend and an acquaintance of Caroline's. She wondered if he had told her, or if she already knew. Was she testing her?

Would this screw up what they had just offered her? Would she be looking for a new job herself instead of looking for someone to step up and replace her? A rush of worry heated her body. She composed herself and gave Caroline a confident expression and a firm tone.

"A lady never talks, but what happened needs to stay there as I have a home life and a family. It was just a one-off, nothing more."

Her voice was steady to the two women, but they could both see the worry etched on her face. They let Robyn's words float along into silence before bursting out with laughter.

"My dear, you need to chill out a bit more!" Caroline assured the now blushing Robyn, as Elizabeth continued to laugh.

"Tell me," Elizabeth stifled her giggles, "is he as good as people say? Caroline's a spoilsport and won't tell me. I am dying to know!"

Relief that she wasn't getting fired washed over Robyn and had brought the colour back to her paled cheeks. Her tone was still serious, her lips forming a hard line.

"All I can say is that it wasn't supposed to happen and won't happen again." Robyn was embarrassed about it because it wasn't, and isn't, the 'done' thing. Her Cheshire grin took both women by surprise as she gushed out,

"But it was fucking amazing. That I will say. I have never been to made feel like that ever, in my entire life. Added to the fact that it wasn't supposed to happen, it just did. I walked in on him in the kitchen and one thing led to the other and yeah… mind-blowing."

Caroline firmly nodded her agreement.

"See, Elizabeth, I told you. I should set it up for you."

"I may just take you up on that offer one day. However, I am fine at the moment."

371

With the conclusion of the meeting and the teasing, they hugged each other and left for the day, leaving the rest of the staff to their work.

Paris was due in town that evening, and Caroline was looking forward to getting glammed up and heading out to the restaurant. Caroline hadn't had the chance to sit down and have a meal with him, ever, and she wanted to catch up with him and see how things were going. She was curious to know if he was still okay with her calling on him when she needed his help with 'things.' She couldn't keep the visions out of her head from the masquerade ball. As the time drew closer to the date, she kept replaying images through her mind. The seductive way they danced, the darkened corner of the room, her sliding down and having him inside her mouth. How he turned her on, how he made her feel, how hard he had taken her. She was craving for his body again. She wasn't too sure if they would make it through dinner before she jumped him right then and there. Caroline had already checked in at the hotel and had an overnight bag in the back of the car.

She arrived in plenty of time and thought about taking a long bath to try to replay the whole ball episode from start to finish. She decided that a relaxing one would suffice instead. This setting was different and wouldn't have the same atmosphere. She didn't want to ruin the memory of being in France, since that was the day she made her decision to alter her lifestyle.

Since France, she had been having quite the adventure, and as she kept it hidden from most, she wanted to make sure every memory would be preserved in perfect condition in her mind. It was interesting to her though, that no matter where her life took her with her fantasies, she kept reverting back to Paris. Yes, she had had amazing times and some wild sex sessions with people, but what he managed to do to her and the way he made her feel was indescribable. He forced her to step outside of her comfort zone, pushed her to her limits, and his body… she craved it all over again.

She took her time getting ready for dinner and knew that he would be sitting at the bar waiting for her. She paid attention to every detail of her ensemble before she left the hotel room. She wanted him drooling over her. Her long hair was ruler-straight, an elegant dress showcasing the curves of her body in all the right places, with just the right amount of skin to make him ache to have her.

The design of the dress itself was simple, yet stunning on her figure. It was a deep shade of purple, had a low, dipping neckline in the front, but not too low. A conservative split at the back made it so that when she walked, you could see her toned legs. Following those legs down, you came to her pointed-toe high-heels, which capped off her head-turning attire.

She arrived at the bar and as she had suspected, he was sitting there waiting. He had

rdered a bottle of red wine, which was open and
breathing on the bar with a glass already poured for
her. He rose from his seat as she approached and
pulled out her chair for her. She graciously accepted
and sat down.

Paris picked up her glass, handed it to her and
made a small toast to the evening. Both took a sip
while keeping eye contact with one another. He looked
a tad nervous to her and she thought she would break
the ice.

"Let's get straight to the point; is this a
full-service date or just dinner with a friend? Or…"
Her red-painted lips curved into a grin, "am I going
to catch you naked in front of my fridge tonight as
well?" As he blanched somewhat, she threw her head
back and laughed.

He knew that Robyn would have told her and
didn't know how she would take it. But, he thought,
as she had sent her over to him in France, it was
expected of him to pleasure her.

After all, she had said that if she set him a task, that he was to complete it with his utmost passion.

Paris relaxed as he could see she was okay with his night with Robyn and eased back into the chair.

"You do know that she was the first married woman I have been with, right?" Caroline raised an eyebrow at his admission as he continued. "To be perfectly honest with you, it was a fantastic night.' He shrugged and sipped his wine.

Caroline turned to him, her eyes narrowed, and she looked at him like she was going to slap him. He froze, worried he'd said too much. She couldn't hold it any longer and burst out laughing.

"Well, at least I know that you do as you are told. It's reassuring to know that you complete all your tasks to their fullest. That is a fine quality in my book."

They chatted before they were shown to their table and continued the conversation about France.

She wanted to know if he knew any other way of closing the deal, like him getting closer to anyone on the inside. He already knew most of the main players in the company, but this wasn't going to be easy as he didn't want to burn all of the contacts he had.

Once word got out that he had been involved in setting it up, people would be standoffish with him and not let him get too close. He understood that they would be afraid he would do the same to them and their companies.

Caroline knew she already had enough to pursue it but would never rest on just what she had. She wanted to make sure that once she stepped into that company, that they saw she had all the facts and that she could help them. Plus, she had an ace in the hole. She'd arranged time with the man on the list, who could be a game-changer. That one meeting could take their fledgeling business to the next level within months of starting up.

She took a sip of her wine.

"Okay, enough about business. Let's enjoy dinner, see where this full-service date goes and how much effort you put into it."

He flashed her a heart-stopping grin. "It's not Paris, but I am sure I can do more things to you, and for you, while we are here. You never said this was a task, but hey, if you want me to give my all and prove to you that I can do all I need to, then just relax, eat your meal and leave the rest of the night to play out the way it is meant to. Nothing will ever go to plan, but if you just let it happen you will get the best of it."

Caroline returned his smile and they both continued their meals and enjoyed each other's company, even though Caroline couldn't get the image out of her mind about the ball and what he could be doing to her right then and there. Her body was aching, and she was longing to be touched by him. She wanted him to just take what he wanted and to satisfy er so badly, she could feel the sexual tension building.

Caroline kept glancing over his body in his fitted, tailored shirt and imagined taking it off him right there in the restaurant and teasing him so much that he would lose control, pick her up and have her on the table. She envisioned plates and glasses flying off the table and smashing on the floor. Wine bottles would be sent flying across the room as he threw her down on the table. How he would rip open her dress, push himself onto her and take her with such force that the table they were on would groan under their movements. She couldn't stop thinking about it; her body was already reacting to what she was thinking, and she knew he could sense it.

She kept thinking about the deal she had made with him, being at her call if she needed help getting information and helping in other ways. She kept running it through her mind. *'Was it okay to do this?'* Women have always been perceived in a sexual nature, and sometimes exploited in that way. She had to remember that he was a willing participant as well, and had jumped in with both feet when he was propositioned. It wasn't as if she was holding anything over his head to do it. He appeared to be enjoying the attention and acted like he was more than happy to do it. She knew that, at some point, he would want to stop and when the time came that he gave the word, she would drop it immediately.

They finished their meal and headed back to the bar for another drink and continued talking about their past and getting to know each other more. Caroline found herself becoming increasingly intrigued by him, his past and how he had got to the place he was at now in his life. He was a strong businessman with a successful vineyard and the body of a Greek god. They could have sat there through the night, drinking and talking, but Caroline was getting more turned on each passing moment. They were sitting close and each time he would move his legs, they would brush against hers. It was starting to drive her crazy. She wanted him.

Caroline turned to him, her voice hushed, heavy with need.

"I think we should take this upstairs now and continue where we left off in Paris." She rose out of the chair, running her fingers along his cheek.

He didn't need another invitation from her, so he stood and escorted her to the lift. As they entered, she was wondering if he would take her like he had in the lift at the hotel in Paris, or if he would wait.

She didn't have to wait long to find out as he moved in closer to her and took her gently into his arms. This was a different feeling for her than before, as he was being tender and sensual with his touches. It was as if he was exploring her neck and body for the very first time, like two lovers that had been thrown together after an eternity apart. He kissed her neck gently with just a brush of his lips against her glowing skin. His warm breath sent shivers racing through her body that could have turned on the most difficult of women to please.

His hold around her waist was light, and he pulled her in closer, not with force but with a tenderness that only two people that close, in deep desire and lust for one another, could ever imagine. The doors opened and she fumbled for her room key and drop it on the floor. He leant down, picked it up and handed it back to her. There was a smile in his eyes, and he knew, deep down, that this was her night, not his. He had led the way in France, but she was the one calling the shots tonight. She was the one that set it up, so he was just following her lead. He wanted her to feel desired and longed for, to have him whichever way she was inclined to, and to be the one that was pleasured beyond the bounds that she had felt before.

Caroline opened the door, held it open for him and motioned for him to enter. Once inside, she closed the door and locked it behind them and dropped er purse on the table. It didn't take long before they started where they had left off in the lift.

Caroline pulled him in closer to her as they stood in the doorway, but with Caroline taking the lead, she kissed him with passion, yet gently explored his lips with her tongue before letting him come in closer for a deeper kiss. They took their time to kiss deeply, being more involved in each other's flicks and touching of their tongues, that that first kiss seemed to last for an age. He was fuelling the fire within her as his hands started to explore her body from the back, grasping her sides. She had one hand on the upper part of his shoulders from under his arm while the other held his head firmly in place as she ran her fingers through his hair.

He lifted her gently around the waist and carried her over to the bed and put her down beside it. The lust in their eyes told the truth about what they both were aching to have. He moved his hands around the back to start to undo her dress when she stopped him. Looking at her, he knew that she was telling him to slow down and to take his time, as they had all night. She took his hands and put them by his side; she was the one making the moves now, as he had had his chance in France and this was her show now. She unbuttoned his shirt and pushed it back over his shoulders by the collar and let it fall gently off his body, making sure to keep a hold of it as she wanted him to wait and feel the tension build up.

She moved away and laid it down on a chair by the bed and walked back over, this time coming up from behind him. Caroline started to kiss his back and shoulders, running her hands the full length of the parts of his body that she had uncovered, making sure to bring his senses and emotions to boiling point.

Her fingers explored every inch of his back before she moved them around the front and held onto his chest while she continued to kiss his back making him flinch with every touch of her lips. Once she had a hold of his chest, she turned her kisses to small

ites sinking in her teeth gently, but not to draw
ny blood from him, but enough so she could feel his
hest rise in her hands and his heart rate increase.

Once she had felt the way he was responding to
er touch and teasing, she lowered her hands down to
is belt and started to undo the buckle, releasing it
nd letting the parts open while she worked on his
utton and his zip. She hadn't moved away from his
ack and wanted him to feel the way she had felt when
he wasn't allowed to touch him back while in Paris.

Her hands entered the top of his trousers and
lid down inside, where they met his swollen and
hrobbing cock within seconds, and she grasped it
ard to feel his heartbeat racing through it. This
as the point she knew that she was the one calling
he shots, she was his master now. She turned him
round and slowly removed his trousers from around
is legs and had him standing there, naked and
hrobbing, in front of her. She couldn't hide her
xcitement and she had longed for it again, but this
as different, no hard, animalistic sex, no throwing

her down and holding her in place, forcing himself inside her and fucking her like she had needed to be taken that night. This was a slow, rich and exuberant growth between two people and an exploration of two luxuriant bodies encapsulated in the heat of the moment.

Caroline was taking her time; she turned him around, put his hands behind his back and clasped them together and looked into his eyes.

"Do not move your hands an inch," she said, her voice thick with passion. She slowly started to kiss his chest and to work on him like he had done to her body. This wasn't payback as such for him teasing her, this was about her having her time, filling her desires and cravings.

The tenderness of her fingers on his skin sent shivers up and down his body in waves. He quaked at her touch and his body responded to each and every movement of her fingertips and tongue on him. She slowly massaged his swollen member with her mouth and

icked his head gently. Every time she slid to the
op, she took as much as she could inside her mouth,
emembering the first time she had the opportunity to
ave him in her mouth and how it felt the first time
e spread her mouth to breaking point.

He was still big to her, but now he was more of
gentle giant with her telling him what to do.
olding her impulse to let him have her, she
ontinued to take in every ridge of his muscles with
er hands, devouring every inch of him inside her
outh and making sure she pushed him further to the
imits of being teased than he had ever gone. She
anted him to explode hard, but also wanted him to be
eld back and wait for when she wanted it.

Caroline's body was also at the edge of
rupting into orgasms, even though she hadn't been
ouched yet and as much as she was enjoying the time
he was spending on him, she desired, more than
nything, his touch on her.

She stood, keeping her hands touching him at all times as she worked her way up to his chest and kissed as much as she could without letting out the sighs of pleasure that she was getting as his swollen cock hit her clit while she rose. It was enough to send her into blissful orgasm, but she held back and took a deep breath. She allowed him to remove his hands and he brought them forward, put them around her as they kissed harder than before. Caroline needed it now. Paris put his hands around her waist and picked her up, still being as gentle as two people so deeply involved in the moment could be. He didn't move from the same spot as he slowly lowered her down onto him. Her body accepted him without a struggle as she engulfed him inside her.

As he lowered her down onto him further, she shuddered as she let the first orgasm rip through her body. She couldn't hold back any longer. His hands moved underneath her as she wrapped her arms around his shoulders and neck. Paris was now in control of his movements but not in control of her will. She was

etting him take her as she was the one that wanted
t. She had let him move and lift her up, but it
asn't for him to decide where and when. It was all
n Caroline's hands; she was allowing him to have
er, and that is what made the difference to her.

Paris hadn't stopped his motions as all the
houghts raced through her mind. He was now lifting
er higher and sliding her down harder onto him and
ith each lift and drop, her body reacted to him. She
as holding on tighter and tighter around his neck
nd her lips were sucking him inside her deeper with
ach of his strokes. He now wasn't just lifting and
ropping her, his hips were in random movements,
oing in circles, then front to back to keep her on
dge.

Her body now was about to be devoured in a
tate of unbridled orgasm when he moved her off his
eck and lowered her backwards leaning away from him
nd the only things now holding her in place were his
trong arms. She couldn't reach up and touch him as
e had leaned her so far back that she could nearly

reach out and touch the floor. He slowly moved her towards the bed until her hands hit the side of it and she managed to grab onto it. He watched as she took a hold of it hard and then started to take the slides in and out of her all over again. Her legs released around his waist and he held her perfectly as the muscles on his arms bulged at the burden of having to balance and hold her in place. This didn't faze him at all, and he started to go deeper and harder into her, taking each stroke like it was the last one, pulling out to the brim and then sliding back in deep and with enough force that she could feel his intent to give her the satisfaction that she was craving. Her body was now pulsating uncontrollably, and each stroke brought new and more intense waves of orgasms. Mini orgasms began to course through her and led to longer, far more body-consuming orgasms that had her screaming and moaning.

He was in complete tune with her body and what she wanted. She wasn't caring now who was in control of what, she just wanted him not to stop.

Paris had no intention of stopping, as he
lifted her up and moved her over the top of the bed
and slowly laid her down, and removed himself from
her. With that movement, she arched her back and
moaned loudly as the last part of him came out of
her.

He wasn't finished at all. He knelt down at the
side of the bed and spread her legs wider again, and
Paris pushed his tongue inside her, engaging a full-
on glass-shattering scream that just made him take
his time and delve deeper inside of her. Caroline was
the perfect person to play with, as she knew her body
and what it needed and how to get someone to do it
for her.

They were so in-tune, and when he touched her
the way her body needed, she made the most erotic
noises. They were intense, simply delicious sounds of
the deepest pleasure. Every time he pushed his tongue
into her, she would moan and wriggle harder and
harder. She took a hold of his head, yanked and

pulled him harder onto her as her body was telling her to do so.

The more he lapped at her flowing juices, the further he wanted to taste her and pleasure her beyond reason. This wasn't about just pleasuring himself; he made sure, as he always did, that he gave as much as he received.

He entered her with one finger, making sure that he explored every inch of her with it so that he could find the perfect spot inside her that would make her screams louder and her orgasms harder. She had long, deep, highly-charged orgasms that just kept building the longer he played with her.

Her body let go and shuddered against his touch, as she felt the passion he had for her and the immense pressure his fingers and tongue were having on her body. She was now aching with each and every touch and he hadn't even entered her yet. She wondered how much more she was going to be able to ake and if he was going to be this intense with her

hile actually inside her.

He eased his playing and took the time to
lance up towards her eyes and see what sort of
ffect he was having on her. Her eyes were wide and
hining in the light streaming through the window
rom the stars and moon. Her breathing was making her
hest rise higher and higher with each stroke of his
ingers and her body was contorting into different
ositions as she had orgasm after orgasm, until they
urned into one long one and she never thought they
ould end. Her body ached, not for him to stop, but
or him to continue his sensual torture. She had
asted so long, she thought to herself, *'What more
ould he do to me that could ever top this?'* She knew
hat he could do from her first experience with him
n Paris, but that was now a thing of the past, as
he present was even more intense than the first
ncounter. Boy, was she to be proved wrong.

Caroline arched her back against him so she
ould feel his immense frame pushed up against her

back. He moved his hands to her breasts and then slowly slid a finger deep inside her again, but it wasn't anything that Caroline wasn't used to from him. He moved his whole body and laid her on top of him, laying her flat against his heaving chest.

He had one of his hands wrapped around her chest and the other hand's fingers were buried deep inside her. She was at his complete submission. He was kissing her neck and biting in between, not enough to draw blood, but hard enough so she would wriggle and push herself down harder onto his fingers. He was lavishing her breasts with such devotion to his task. His thumb gently stroked and played with her clit and tender spots.

Her head rolled back onto him and her eyes rolled back in her head. He had brought her so close to her body erupting in ecstasy. The power and control he had over her body were building and he was not just stimulating her deep inside, but her whole body was reacting to each and every touch.

To her it was mind-blowing; her body was going to be driven to the uppermost level of orgasms. She knew that once he had her at that point, she wasn't going to be able to hold back. Her body would be at his mercy and the way he was going, she knew he couldn't just stop there. If he did stop, she knew she would be begging for more even though she didn't know how much she would be able to take.

Her body was contorted into positions that it had not been put into before. The first electrically charged orgasm hit and she couldn't fight it. Her sweet spot was aching as her body let go. Without being able to scream or speak, she came again, groaning as every inch of her body tensed and every muscle was as taut as it could be. It was like she hadn't ever had it like this before. it was

getting to the point where it was too much for her body to take. Caroline couldn't wait any longer; she needed to feel him inside her. It had been a long time since the ball, and she was craving to be filled.

She yearned to feel him, she wanted to feel the pressure he would put inside her again, like at the beginning of the night, every inch of him filling up every part of her. She wanted to feel like there was nothing left of her, just him inside her.

He turned her over, but he wasn't done yet. He wanted to taste her, but she had other plans. As he started to explore the rest of her body all over again, she reached out and grabbed his swollen member and slid it right into her mouth. She wasn't letting him take complete control. She wanted him to know that even though she was craving him, she was also making sure she had her play time as well. She made it clear that she could tease him just as much as he was doing to her.

She flipped him onto his back and started to take her time, taking every thick inch of him in her hand, playing with him, tasting him inside her as she took both her hands and started to run them up and down his shaft. Her fingers grasped him tightly and started to stroke harder and firmer on his now rock-

olid cock. She knew now was the time to have him
egging for more as her body was starting to relax a
ittle bit, and once she had him to the point of no
eturn, she would be able to tease and calm him down.
hen she planned to take what she ultimately wanted…
im deep inside of her.

She kept up the motion of her hands and she
ould feel him shaking in her grip, the relentless
ovement of her hands and her lips firmly around him,
er tongue running the length of his shaft and head,
rawing every inch of him to swell harder and reach
reaking point. She could make him explode without
oo much more, but she wanted to savour the moment,
eep it going as long as she could, payback for
aking her body ache as much as he did without giving
er what she wanted the most.

She had him at her mercy and on his back. He
ay have been twice the size of her, but she wasn't
iving an inch back. She slowed down and kept a hold
f him so he couldn't move. With every twitch of her
ongue on him, she sent him into spasms that

stretched from head to toe. She was still longing for him to be inside her, but she wasn't ready to give in to what he wanted as well.

He tried to move, and she sank her teeth into the base of him while he was deep inside her mouth and he had no more control as his body shot out the first specimen of cum inside her. She didn't miss a stroke and continued as she had started, not losing a drop and tasting him all the way down.

He grabbed her head and the second heavier round shot out of him like a bullet. It hit the back of her throat and made her take a deep breath before continuing.

Caroline knew that she wouldn't be able to stop now and would have to continue until he was ready to be mounted or for him to take her, even though he hadn't been inside of her again. Her body had already been satisfied more than any other had managed since her trip to the ball. He reached down and grabbed her head gently as he couldn't contain what she had been

oing to him and wouldn't be able to continue much
ore as he was just as tender down there now as well.

Caroline wasn't used to not getting what she
anted, but she also knew that she had made him as
appy and satisfied as he had made her already. Just
ecause they hadn't had full-on sex on more than one
ccasion, didn't mean that they had not got what they
oth desired and wanted.

Caroline and Paris were both breathing heavily,
heir bodies having been taken hard without being
riven to the full extent. They collapsed beside each
ther, not knowing what would happen next. All they
new was that, at that moment, they were both where
hey were meant to be. The had been connected after
he ball in such a way that they just kept getting
rawn closer to each other.

Caroline got up, had a shower and changed. She
alked back to the room and Paris was asleep on the
ed like he had been in France. She decided to leave
im the same note as before. She quietly left her

gentle giant and headed back to her home to relax for

the weekend.

Chapter 16.
Pushing Forward

Caroline spent the weekend relaxing and doing the odd bit of work, as she knew that the meeting coming up would be something that they needed to hit perfectly if they were to get to the front of the line with the business in Europe.

She knew that Elizabeth would be doing the same, and with the work she did on the background research, this would be a meeting they could be proud of. Nothing they had done before this deal would count, as this would be the major event that would put everything into perspective to build their business.

She spent the night going from business meetings' agendas to looking back on the night before. She could still feel everything inside her body that he had done to her, and what she had done to him.

Caroline's phone rang and it was Alicia. She told Caroline she had more information for her on a couple of the people in the Europe deal and would

email it to her. Caroline was thrilled about that, a
she was doing research and said she looked forward t
getting it. Alicia was enthusiastic about that and
said that she had had to postpone her weekend away
for a few weeks as this was more important. She
stated that the spa manager knew about it and would
accommodate the new dates she needed to change to and
just to get back to them when she could.

Caroline told her it was no problem and thanked
her. She asked for Alicia to let her know the dates
she would be away so that she knew not to disturb
her. Alicia agreed and said goodnight. Caroline knew
that she would have to inform her guest to cancel the
next weekend and that she would let him know the
rescheduled dates as soon as she knew them.

Monday morning came and she picked up the phone
and waited for Elizabeth to answer her call.

"I have had an email, and we have a meeting
set, are you ready?" She could hear Elizabeth smiling
through the phone.

"I have never been so ready for a meeting in my entire life."

"Excellent! I will pick you up in your lobby in an hour. I'll grab the coffee and we will have breakfast and then we will head out. Make sure Robyn is there as well."

Caroline put down the phone and smiled. *'This is what we have been working towards.'* Even though they had been only going for a little over two months, she had been dreaming of this kind of moment for most of her working life; The one meeting that would build her own business. Nothing meant more to her now than this, and it wasn't just her life now, it was Elizabeth's as well.

They were depending on each other more than ever. It was the time to see what they were both capable of and what they were willing to do to get the deal of a lifetime. What would they be willing to give up? What would something like this cost them?

'*Only time will tell.*' She had pushed her personal life's boundaries so far now that she couldn't see them, and she loved it. Now it was time to do the same with the business, pushing forward on what she could do and what she could accomplish.

She knew the profession, so did Elizabeth, and together she knew that they could bring business deals to the table and make their clients know that they could help them and change things for the better.

Caroline was already set to leave, but had to make sure she gave them time to get ready and be ready to be picked up. She called down and made sure her driver was ready and made her way down. She would be early, but Elizabeth lived not too far away, and she knew that she would be ready by the time she got there. It just depended on how quick Robyn could get organised and be ready. They had dropped it on her at short notice and realised she had kids to get ready and didn't want to put so much pressure on her that she lost all train of thought when they were sorting

ut what they needed to bring up in the meeting. The
ast thing they needed was for Robyn's mind to wander
nto whether or not she had got all of the kids'
tuff ready for school and or forgotten anything.

Caroline called Robyn, who answered after the
hird ring. Caroline thought she sounded confident
nd ready.

"You know we are getting together for breakfast
nd we all have a meeting to attend, however, do not
ush. It is not until this afternoon. We will have a
ong breakfast and I will send a car for you. Again,
o not rush at all, take whatever time you need to.
e can eat when you get there. My driver will just
ait for you for as long as he is needed to." This
as music to Robyn's ears, but she assured Caroline
hat she wasn't going to let her down.

"Thank you so much, Caroline. I am almost
eady, and I feel great about today. I'll be ready
hen your driver gets here."

Caroline arrived to pick up Elizabeth and let her know that once they got to the place where they were going to have breakfast, her driver was going to go and pick up Robyn. She stated they would wait for her before they ate breakfast, but they could indulge themselves with coffee until she arrived.

Coffee, for both of them, was the staple of the morning. If they could have had it pumped directly into their veins, they would have been in the front of the line every morning for the IV hook-up.

They sat and chatted for a while about their weekends and Caroline told her that she had met up with Paris on Friday night and that she left him again with the same note as she had left him in the hotel in France.

They joked about it and had a few more things to say about that night, but Caroline didn't want to give out too many details, as she was sure at some stage, Paris was going to want to seduce Elizabeth ithout her setting them up. She knew that Elizabeth ouldn't be able to resist him if it came down to it.

Robyn arrived about twenty minutes later and rdered a large coffee with a double shot inside to atch herself up with the morning. She was sure that he other two were on their second cup already. She at down, they all ordered breakfast, then they tarted to talk about the upcoming meeting.

"We don't need to go into too much detail here. ust make sure we are on the same page. Robyn, you re here not just to sit and watch, you know the ins nd outs of this, and you will know if what the guy s saying is right or not. Do not be worried about topping him in his tracks. We want him to know that e have researched the details and know what we are alking about. Remember, this is yours to run with. lizabeth and I will steer him in the right direction nd once he is there, we will need all the nformation laid out." Caroline sipped her coffee, hile Robyn fidgeted slightly.

"It's a one-shot deal here; we have one try at this, One chance to make an impact, one effort to land this deal. If he is on board and likes the figures we are giving him, then we will have his backing."

Robyn nodded. Her stomach was doing flip-flops, but she was more excited than nervous.

"Don't worry, Caroline, I have all the numbers and the emails you forwarded to me from Alicia as well, and I have everything we need."

Caroline glanced at Elizabeth, then back at Robyn.

"I have faith in both of you. We *can* get this pushed through. The trust I have in Elizabeth to pul me back if she needs to, and the utmost trust I have in your hard work ethic, Robyn, is strong. Solid. I have no doubt that this will be all we need to make this happen." The ladies raised their coffee mugs in cheers. Their breakfast arrived with more coffee and hey sat enjoying the time they had and halted urther business discussion for the morning.

Caroline knew Elizabeth would step in, if eeded, and throw so much at him when the time came, hat he wouldn't have a choice but to trust them and o go with what they said. It all made sense as the igures don't lie; the amount of finance needed was efty, but they had the banks' backing. The profits hat could be had would be more than he could refuse.

When it came to business, Caroline knew that oney talked in their world, but most of all, a track ecord with making money on every single deal she had ade, combined with her team behind her, meant othing was going to stop them trying their best.

They finished the meal, headed out to the car nd left for the meeting.

About an hour later, they arrived at a set of arge iron gates that led to the massive house on the utskirts of London and pulled up to the speaker box.

The driver called through on the intercom and the gates opened.

This was it; the lengthy driveway twisting up to the house, flanked on both sides by old trees tha covered the road, was all that stood between them an the deal of a lifetime. They rounded the last corner and the house came into view in the distance. It was an old country home that had been given a new lease on life and was a sight to behold. It was like something out of a magazine, or classic novel. They all openly gawked at it as they drove closer.

The women looked at each other and could tell they were all thinking the same thing. One meeting, one shot, one chance. They were the only ones that had their futures on the line in front of them. It was the three women alone, and no one else, that could make this happen.

They pulled up at the front door of the house and gazed out the window.

It was in their hands now…

To be continued

Just the start

She stood proud

As she recalled a woman from some time ago

A woman driven by an unsatiated hunger

A woman yearning for sinful satisfaction

Now, she is a woman changed

Her demons had been pounded

and some had been embraced

Fantasies were brought to fruition

Delectable appetites had been filled

Yet, deep within her belly, she still found yearning

She stood in wanting

Knowing that her journey had just begun

That she was on the cusp of discovering her deepest desires

She was ready to let them unfold

And nibble on the savoury morsels that lie in waiting

It was time to broaden her palate

To dip and careen into unchartered territories

Sampling all that will fill her voracious flavours

She stood in heated fervour

As the white heat flowed from her erect nipples

To the warmth ruminating from between her thighs

Allowing her own fingers to explore the sticky juices

Dripping from her throbbing lips

A smile forming as she brought her delicate digits to

Her red-lipped smile, tasting her own juices

With sweltering vehement pleasure

She stood in alacrity

Free from all reservation

Her body and her sex proffered to the world

She was anew, alive, and had been reborn

The woman, now changed, with one story concluded, but take heed...

For a new chapter has begun...

Witness...Follow...Embark...

415

She stood unmoving

By Robin LeOra

Lightning Source UK Ltd.
Milton Keynes UK
UKHW020617211219
355800UK00013B/368/P